Uncrossing Her Legs

This is a work of fiction. Names, character, places and incidents are products of the author's imagination or are used fictitiously. Any resemblance to actual events or locales or persons, living or dead, is entirely coincidental.

ISBN-13: 978-0982657096

ISBN 13: 978-0982657096

PRINTED IN THE UNITED STATES OF AMERICA

Uncrossing Her Legs

A Novel

Teresa D. Patterson

Chapter One

"Damn," Dominique Green swore, sucking air through her teeth in frustration. She took off her Gucci shades in order to stare down at the ruined shoe. She should have taken it as a premonition when the heel of her $250 pump snapped, causing her ankle to twist, as she got ready to get into her silver, SLK-Class Mercedes Benz.

She wasn't going to worry about it though. Being equipped to handle such situations, (because a lady is *always* prepared) she pulled the lever and the trunk popped open. She got out, walked around to the back of the car and promptly selected another pair of shoes out of the built-in, custom shoe rack. She would never be caught slipping. A woman has to always have a backup plan. That goes for any situation.

Though her ankle throbbed, upon inspection she saw that it wasn't swollen. Satisfied that the shoes matched her trendy Dolce & Gabbana skirt set she slid her feet into them. Dominique frowned at the damaged shoe that she'd taken off. She tossed the set into the back of the trunk, slamming the lid shut. Glancing at her gold diamond encased watch she frowned slightly.

She still had enough time to make a grand entrance. She just knew that everyone on her floor would be waiting to honor her. This marked the first day she'd be stepping into her new job position as Account Executive at Troutman Mutual Funds and Investments. And step is exactly what she intended to do— more like strut.

She'd pretend to be shocked when her co-workers yelled out, "Surprise!" She was good at being fake and phony. Hell, she'd had enough practice over the years.

She smiled as she headed in the direction of the office, not even letting the congested morning traffic irritate her as it usually did. It was a nice morning, warm enough to profile. She'd let down her drop-top if she weren't afraid of messing up her new weave job. She couldn't let a $200 up-do blow in the wind, no matter how tempting.

Driving five miles over the speed limit, Dominique let her mind set the scene. She could almost bet that her secretary, Brenda, had ordered balloons and the likes. There'd be a big, decorated cake filled to the capacity with calories, the last thing her hips needed. Confetti could litter the top of her new desk. That would the cherry wood oak desk she'd ordered to her specifications, with matching filing cabinets. As the new Account Executive, Dominique had her office completely redecorated. Mr. Troutman had spared no expenses. When it came to getting things to go her way, Dominique was a pro.

It didn't take long before she arrived at her destination. She found a parking space close to the building and pulled into it. For the umpteenth time, she wished her parking arrangements had been worked out so that she could be under the covered garage. Her baby didn't need to be out in the open so birds could shit on it. Besides, some jealous bitch she'd probably pissed off could key it up, since it was easy to spot. If she could park under the covered garage, the camera would give her a sense of security.

She would have to work on Marcus regarding that. He was in charge of the assigned parking. Maybe it was time she took him up on that offer of a date. He asked her at every chanced opportunity. The problem with Marcus was he wasn't up to her standards. Marcus prided himself for being head of security, but in Dominique's opinion, that wasn't good enough. She doubted that his paychecks for an entire month could cover her rent. Any man she associated with had to have something going for them career wise. There would be no sponging off of her.

She had to admit, Marcus was fine. She smiled as she pictured his chocolate, smooth skin and unusual hazel eyes. He stood around six three, with a well-built, solid frame. He had arms the size of Dwayne "The Rock" Johnson. She'd have to think about hooking up with him and weigh whether or not if it was worth parking under the covered garage.

Still smiling, she stepped through the automatic doors of Troutman Mutual Funds

3

and Investments. Not hearing, "Surprise!" as she'd expected, caused her plastered on fake smile to waver. Where were all the people? Where was the noise and the excitement associated with a celebration? All she encountered was an "I can hear a pin drop" type of quietness.

"Good morning, Ray," she said to the security guard posted at the front desk. Ray, usually cheerful and animated, sat wearing a glum expression on his haggard face. He looked up and she could have sworn that his bottom lip trembled.

Damn. Something bad must have happened, Dominique thought.

"Not such a good morning, Miss Green. Mr. Troutman died. Just fell over his desk. Heart attack, I suspect," Ray revealed.

"Oh no," she exclaimed, more so for herself than for Mr. Troutman. She really did feel bad that he'd kicked the bucket, but she felt even worse because now nobody would be thinking about her. A heart attack certainly would put a damper on celebrating her success.

She could tell that Ray waited for some words of comfort or consolation. Searching down deep inside, she found nothing to offer him. Instead, she hurried to catch the elevator. "See you later," she threw out. Ray's shoulders hunched in grief, but Dominique didn't catch it because the elevator doors closed.

UNCROSSING HER LEGS

Feeling somewhat deflated, she pushed the button for the third floor. As she waited to arrive at her destination, she tried not to pout. Maybe Brenda had something planned. She shouldn't have expected to be greeted by the entire company. She wasn't the president or even the CEO for that matter.

Dominique Green was spoiled and selfish. She knew it and everyone who was anyone knew it too. Her selfishness didn't stop men from going out of their way to accommodate her, though. She could also woo most of the women she encountered, on a good day. Nothing got in the way of her getting what she wanted. Today, she wanted a cake and some balloons damn-it. Today might be the first time she didn't get her way, and that thought made her livid.

The elevator stopped on the second floor and a drop dead gorgeous, black Adonis got on. Dominique quickly checked her reflection in the shiny interior of the elevator's walls. She looked chic, as usual. She made it a habit to always be on point. She had every hair in place, make-up immaculate, and nails French manicured down with the toes to match.

The gentleman barely acknowledged her as he leaned in to push three. Seeing that the button was already lit, he settled against the far wall.

"Good morning," Dominique tried.

"Um," he mumbled.

Who shoved a sour lemon up your ass this morning? She wondered. She thought about just letting this one go but out the corner of her eye she could see that he had it going on. His fine physique immediately made her panties moist.

He was tall, dark and handsome in every sense of the word. He stood at least six foot six. He carried himself well beneath his Armani suit. His shoes proved that he had good taste as well as money. A Kmart salary couldn't afford such a sharp wardrobe. He even had the bling bling to match. A 24 karat gold necklace draped his neck. He sported a diamond earring in both lobes. They were real diamonds not Cubic Zirconium. She checked out his Rolex watch and took in the perfectly manicured fingernails. That turned her on even more. In her opinion, a grown ass man with oil and dirt under his fingernails had to be the most disgusting sight ever.

She kept taking inventory of the gentleman. His hair wasn't to her liking. She preferred a brother to wear a low cut fade. This brother sported dreadlocks. They appeared to be soft and inviting to the touch. Plus, they looked clean and not like some bird's nest or matted yarn.

The brother was definitely up on his hygiene. In her opinion, that was important. Nine times out of ten, if a man looked dirty, then the seat of his drawers would probably be crusty or he'd be ashy. That was definitely a turnoff.

Thinking about ashy people took Dominique back to one of her past flings. Melvin Wilson would dress in the best clothes that money could buy. Sean Jean, Roc A Wear, G Unit: a name brand accompanied anything he owned. The downside, he'd be wrinkled from head to toe like an elephant. To make matters worse, he'd be ashy. His elbows and ankles resembled miniature chalkboards. He hadn't the slightest clue that no lotion makes you dry sometime. To top it off, the brother's armpits must have been afraid of deodorant. She'd been sad to see the money go, but her nostrils hadn't been able to put up with Melvin for more than three months.

And his feet. She wouldn't be surprised if he could walk on hot coals. He needed a special kind of foot soak for those bear claw replicas. He needed to go old school with it and just add some Epsom salt and a cap full of bleach in a gallon of hot water. That would scald the husk right off of them bad boys.

Thinking about Melvin's feet made her laugh out loud. She couldn't contain herself.

"Am I amusing you?" The deep, rich tones of the stranger's voice rushed over her like a caress. Dominique had forgotten that she wasn't alone. She quickly cleared her throat.

"Oh, no. Not at all. I was just thinking about something," she said, still giggling from the image of Melvin holding a bottle of Clorox.

"Well, at least someone can find humor on a day like this." He glanced her way. "Mr. Troutman just died, or did you hear the news yet?"

"I was informed when I arrived," she stated, pulling herself together and switching to business mode. "I'm heading to his office now. By the way, I'm his new Account Executive," she added.

"Oh? Well, you must be grief-stricken?" His eyes met hers and narrowed, suddenly. He'd heard all about his uncle's new Account Executive. A friend of his, Lauretta, worked in the New Accounts department. She'd been more than happy to fill him in on his uncle's excursions. Learning of some of his uncle's business decisions had prompted him to come for a visit. He was glad that he'd had a chance to see his uncle before his death. Was this woman somehow responsible for the heart attack that had taken his uncle away?

His lips curled in distaste at the thought. Lauretta had painted Dominique Green as a headhunter, a self-centered hussy and heartless slut. He was face-to-face with the gold-digger who had slept her way to the top, using his uncle in the process. How ironic for them to meet on the elevator today of all days.

"Grief-stricken?" She gazed at him as though he was delirious. "Not really. I barely knew the man," she said carelessly.

"I'm heading to his office as well." His brown eyes swept over her in a contemptuous

8

glare. "By the way, my name is Arvind Thompson. I'll be stepping in for Mr. Troutman, *my uncle*," he said pointedly.

Dominique's mouth dropped open on its own accord. This was Mr. Troutman's nephew. Oops. She'd spoken her mind as usual. Today, it might have caused her to become ostracized. She had to be more careful. She didn't need a new enemy. She already had enough backstabbers to contend with. If anything, since Arvind would be the new CEO, she needed him in her corner. What was a good way to suck up to him?

She quickly recovered from her initial shock and cleared her throat again. "Mr. Thompson. Arvind, did you say? That's a unique name. I haven't properly introduced myself. I'm Dominique Green." She extended her hand, which he ignored. Feeling slighted, she let it drop back to her side.

They came to a stop and the doors opened. The two of them watched paramedics roll the body of Mr. Troutman onto the elevator.

"Oh my God," Dominique gasped, stepping hurriedly out of the compartment.

"Don't worry Miss Green," Arvind said sarcastically, following her slowly. "The dead can't talk. Your secrets are safe."

For now, he thought.

Of course, Dominique's first day as Account Executive had been ruined. She spent the majority of it accepting condolences from well-wishing co-workers and clients who'd heard of Mr. Troutman's untimely demise.

By lunchtime she'd decided to call it quits. She grabbed her Louis Vuitton purse from the bottom of the desk drawer in preparation to leave. She had to get out of this sad, dismal place before she threw herself over the balcony. Everybody behaved as though Mr. Troutman had been the Reverend Jesse Jackson or Al Sharpton. She'd never witnessed people carry on so. Groups had huddled together talking in hushed tones. People had burst into tears. She'd even seen a few women crying at their desks.

"Miss Green, can I see you in my uncle's office?" She heard from behind, causing her to twirl around in the chair, alarmed.

"What now?" she wondered aloud.

The morning had consisted of a department meeting. Arvind had talked to the department and informed them about paid grief counseling, courtesy of the company. He'd even suggested that if they needed to take the day off in order to deal with the tragedy, they'd still receive pay. He hadn't extended the invitation to Dominique, however. As a matter of fact, he'd basically ignored her the entire morning. Now, he wanted to talk and she just wanted to leave. Not caring to make waves, she got up and followed him.

UNCROSSING HER LEGS

"Have a seat," he offered. She sat down in the gray straight-backed office chair then crossed her legs. Arvind didn't let the movement go unnoticed.

His eyes took in Dominique Green—all of her. She oozed femininity. She was far from being considered beautiful, in his opinion, but she was extremely attractive. Her honey colored skin shone from too much makeup. She could do without that goop caked on her face. It would probably take about five years off her age, too. She had nice, full, Angelina Jolie type lips. Of course, she'd spread some chocolate colored lipstick across them, covering their natural moistness. She had high cheekbones, which added to her striking appearance. Her long graceful neck supported a diamond stud necklace with matching earrings that swung from her lobes. His eyes dropped lower to scrutinize the rest of her. He couldn't tell what size breasts she had because of the thickness of her jacket. He guessed they were a 36 B: not too big, not to small, just the right size to put in your mouth.

Yes, Miss Green was sexy as hell. She crossed her long, shapely legs and he stared at the silky nylons in fascination. He'd love to reach under that little skirt she had on and slide those stockings down her golden thighs, spread her legs and ease one finger inside her. He wondered if she would be as wet as he imagined her to be. How would she taste?

11

"Mr. Thompson, can we get on with it?" Her voice snapped him out of his fantasy. He blinked a few times and stared at her shoes in an effort to not give away his lucid thoughts. Being behind a desk had its advantage: she wasn't able to see how excited he'd become.

"Are those Giovanna?" he asked.

"Excuse me?" She gave him an incredulous stare.

"Your shoes? Are they Giovanna?" he repeated. Now he had Dominique intrigued. Either the brother was one classy man or he was straight up gay.

"No, actually, they're from Kimora Lee Simmons' new line. But I know you didn't call me in here to discuss shoes," she said exasperated.

"You're right." He leaned back in his chair but continued to assess her. After what seemed like a full minute of him ogling her, he spoke. "Miss Green, the nature of this meeting is to inform you that for the next month, we'll be working in close proximity on the Lauderdale account. This is one of our most important clients, if not the most important. We can't afford to let my uncle's death cause us to lose them." He was all seriousness even though the thought of banging her back out clouded his mind. He had to dispel those thoughts from his head. Dominique Green was unnerving him, but he had to gain control. After all, she might be the reason that his uncle's heart had given out. "I understand

that today is your first day as Account
Executive. Well, now you'll get to experience
hard work. From what I've heard about you so
far, that's not something you're accustomed
to." He held up his hand to stop her protest of
outrage. "Don't bother to feign insult. Now is
the time to lay all of the cards on the table. If
you thought that this was going to be an easy
paycheck for you, you've been disillusioned."
He settled back in his uncle's leather chair
and stared at her with hard eyes. "I don't
know the nature of the relationship you may
or may not have had with my uncle. But ours
will be strictly professional. If you can't handle
the job or the extra duties I've assigned, now
is the time to make that clear. I can easily put
you back into your old position. No harm done
and no hard feelings. Mike Parham would be
the ideal replacement-"

"What?" she nearly spat. She'd been silent
up until this point. Now her face contorted in
anger as she uncrossed her legs and leaned
forward in the seat to glare at him. She placed
her hands on the edge of his desk for support.
"Mike Parham doesn't know his asshole from
a donut hole," she snarled.

"Miss Green, this is a professional working
environment. Need I remind you to refrain
from such language?" he asked. "It's offensive.
Besides, it's unbecoming for a lady."

She blew air through her flaring nostrils.
"What's unbecoming is you and your holier
than thou attitude. You waltz in here one day

and you've already formed an opinion of me based on idle gossip. That's unfair," she pointed out.

He rolled his eyes at her and smirked. "Haven't you heard the saying, life is unfair? I'm sure my uncle is thinking that from wherever it is he's gone. He didn't count on dying right at the moment that his company was one of the leading investment firms in the state, did he?" She made it a point to ignore his question. It wasn't as if he'd expected an answer anyway.

"Mr. Thompson, can I go now? You've made it perfectly clear what is expected of me. I'll do my job and give a hundred and ten percent. The Lauderdale account won't suffer. Mike Parham wouldn't know how to handle anything concerning this client since I am the one who signed them in the first place." She sat back in the chair and re-crossed her legs.

Arvind pursed his lips. He had more to say but it could wait. Little did she know, but the days of Miss. Green crossing and uncrossing her legs in her short, sexy, expensive skirts were over. He'd be implementing a new dress code, effective immediately. All women had to wear pants suits or skirts that were three inches above the knee. He could not let lust led him astray. He had a job to do and was determined to succeed at it.

Miss Green was indeed a very desirable woman, but he wasn't falling into her clutches. He knew all about women using

14

what they had to get what they wanted. They crossed his path all the time. Plus, she may have killed his uncle.

"You can go," he told her and she stood up abruptly and made for the door. "One other thing," his words halted her but she didn't turn around. "I expect you to be here at seven tomorrow morning."

"But my shift doesn't start until eight," she said, finally turning to face him.

"I know. But I need someone to make the coffee," he said casually. "It'll probably take you thirty minutes to figure out where to find the coffee pot and another thirty minutes to make it."

Her face stiffened and her eyes narrowed at his obvious insult. Her lips grew tight with ill-concealed anger. "I don't make coffee, Mr. Thompson. That's Brenda's job. I think you need to familiarize yourself with my job duties and responsibilities. I'm nobody's little do-girl," she snapped. "I'll see you tomorrow – at eight." With that, she stalked out of the office. She had too much dignity to let the door slam behind her even though she felt like slamming it so hard that it rocked off the hinges.

Arrvind watched as she sashayed away. Sister was wearing the hell out of that short skirt. That's the reason he *had* to change the dress code. How could he walk around and expect to be taken serious if he had a hard on pressing against the front of his trousers? That could definitely pave the way for

numerous sexual harassment lawsuits, as
well.

Chapter Two

Dominique decided that she'd compromise and be at the office at 7:30. That meant she had to rush in applying her make-up and she'd skipped breakfast. She didn't mind not eating though. She'd make up for it during lunchtime.

When she arrived at the office, she found that neither Mr. Thompson nor Brenda had made it in. It turned out that she had to make the coffee after all. A quarter 'til eight, Brenda called to say she couldn't make it in to work. She explained that her seven-year-old son had suffered an asthma attack. She'd probably need the rest of the week off to care for him. She mentioned something about having to put him on some machine and giving him medications every four hours.

Dominique hung up, glad that she didn't have any brats to contend with. If they came out having asthma, they'd probably needed expensive medications. Children *always* needed something. If it wasn't formula, it was pampers. They graduated on to needing clothes and shoes. If they were bucked toothed, they needed braces. Before long, they wanted cars and houses. She'd be damned if she would spend *her* money on anybody except herself. Nope, kids were out of the question.

"Good morning, Miss Green." Hearing Arvind's voice nearly caused her to drop the cup of steaming coffee she'd just finished pouring.

"Good morning, Mr. Thompson," she managed. "I have your coffee here, if you tell me how you'd like it." She rushed on to say, "Brenda called in. She'll most likely be out the remainder of the week."

"I hope she's alright," he said in concern.

"She's fine. Her son has asthma," she explained. She saw the compassion cloud his eyes. So, he had a heart after all.

"Umff! That's awful. I'll have to give her a call and check on his condition. Not being able to breathe is no joke." He seemed far away all of a sudden.

"Mr. Thompson?" Her voice broke into his thoughts.

"Oh, I'm sorry. I tend to let my mind drift from time to time," he said.

"Here's your coffee. Do you take it with cream and sugar or just plain?"

He stared at the cup that she'd extended towards him. For a second, he'd let his guard down. He couldn't allow that to happen again. This was Dominique Green, the man-eater he was dealing with, after all. It would do him good to always remember that.

He took the Styrofoam cup filled with liquid.

"I apologize, Miss Green. I don't drink the stuff. Never got used to the taste." To her utter

18

amazement, he dropped the beverage into a nearby garbage can. The door to his office closed on her shocked expression.

In her office, Dominique fumed for the first thirty minutes. How dare he waste her time? She had a mind to storm into his office and tell him to kiss her ass. She really had to convince herself not to do anything that could cause her to lose her job. That man infuriated her. But no matter how much of a pompous ass he was, she'd remain professional. She would not let an anal retentive asshole like Arvind make her lose something she'd worked so hard to gain.

Dominique walked over to the file cabinet and snatched open the top drawer. She grabbed some files that she'd been working on the day before. She slammed them on the top of her desk and sat down heavily. She wanted to scream her rage.

Behind the closed door, Arvind chuckled. He could hear Dominique in the next room having a temper tantrum. She'd be okay. She probably considered him to be her worst nightmare.

He really wasn't as anal retentive as he no doubt appeared to be in Dominique's eyes. He just wanted to get his point across. He would not succumb to her overtures, so there was no need for her to make any.

He was almost one hundred percent certain that any interest she may have had in him had dissipated with the coffee incident. If that didn't do the trick, his next deed certainly would.

He pushed the intercom button on his phone to summon Dominique.

"Miss Green?"

"Yes?" Her tone was crisp since she couldn't quite hide her emotions.

"I have an important memo that needs to be sent out immediately. Since Brenda isn't here, I'll need you to type it. Can you come into my uncle's... my office, please?"

"I'll be right there."

"Thank you."

The memo concerned the implementation of the new dress code. Even though Dominique frowned as she typed his dictation, she said nothing. Once finished, she got up to leave.

"I guess that means you can retire that outfit to your closet," he commented. He surveyed the trendy two-piece that she'd chosen to wear. "Or you can save it for club attire." Though she wanted to hurl a comeback at him, she just bit her tongue and kept silent. She did, however, roll her eyes. "Thank you Miss Green. After lunch, report back to my office so that we can go over the Lauderdale account together."

"No problem."

"Oh, before I forget, do you have Brenda's number? I want to call her before I get too engrossed in work." She recited the number to him and he jotted it down on a Sticky

Notepad. "Thank you." He'd already lifted the
receiver and began dialing. "You're
dismissed," he stated, not bothering to glance
her way. "Hello Brenda? This is Mr.
Thompson-" She pulled the door closed softly,
though once again she wanted to slam it.

"*You're dismissed,*" she mimicked. He'd
treated her like she was some damned second
grader in elementary school. Once again, Mr.
Thompson had her blood boiling. She knew
exactly what needed to be done in order to
calm her nerves that were now shot.

She retrieved her cell phone from her
Coach bag and searched through her contact
numbers. She looked for one name in
particular.

Chad.

Chad could help her get her mind right.
She dialed his number and arranged a mid-
day rendezvous.

Chad waited as Dominique got out of her
car. Looking thuggish, yet sexy, in his South
Pole urban wear, for some reason, he
appealed to her. She'd met him at her college
roommate's wedding reception a few months
prior. He'd been confident without being too
cocky, so she gave him her number.

She was so glad that she hadn't ignored
him. He hadn't been the type that usually
attracted her. However, he'd had a certain
confidence that had pulled her in. She called
him a few weeks later and they hooked up.

TERESA D. PATTERSON

The size of his dick had impressed her and the fact that he knew how to work it impressed her even more. Never had she expected a slim man to be so well-endowed. She'd been prepared for Chad to act like a caveman in the bedroom, but he'd surprised her in that aspect as well. He was tender, taking it slow until she'd loosened up. He even allowed her to take full control. She'd liked that most of all.

Though she'd planned to "stick and move," her plans changed the first time he caused her to experience back-to-back orgasms. Chad definitely was a keeper.

"What's up?" he greeted.

"I need some stress relief," she told him, quickly ushering him inside. She barely gave him time to close the door before she was on him. Her hands snatched at his clothes, tugging them off impatiently. He did the same. As soon as she undressed, his hot mouth was on her breasts.

"You need this?"

"Yes," she moaned, as he licked a trail down her stomach. "Forget the foreplay, just fuck me," she commanded.

"Okay." She heard a Magnum pack tear and urged him to hurry up, put it on, and fuck her.

And that's exactly what he did. Bending her over, he took her right in the middle of the living room. He slid in and out of her, making her gasp her pleasure aloud.

22

UNCROSSING HER LEGS

"Oh Chad, fuck this pussy!" Dominique screamed. She couldn't think of anything except his dick going in and out of her.

"Is this what you want?" He grabbed her hips and pulled her back against his powerful thrusts. They could hear the sound of her ass cheeks smacking against his thighs.

"Oh, it feels good! It feels so good. Give it to me!" After a few more thrusts, she felt an intense orgasm wash over her. "Yes! That's it Chad. I'm coming! Do it, baby! I'm coming!" It wasn't long before her legs gave out and she slipped to the carpeted floor. Chad turned her over and put her trembling legs over his shoulders. He drove into her until she shuddered through another climax.

"Damn! I'm 'bout to bust it, baby. Shit!" he swore, as he throbbed and pulsated inside her until he came.

The two lay on the floor until their breathing resumed to normal.

"So, how much time you got to kill?" he asked.

"As much time as it takes."

He grabbed her hands. "You willin' to let me make you lose control?" His eyes challenged her as he reached for the pantyhose she'd shed with the rest of her clothes.

"Yeah, sure." Their eyes held as he used the pantyhose to tie her hands together over her head.

"You won't be disappointed," he promised.

23

Hooking up with Chad had been just what she needed. As she headed back to Troutman Mutual Funds & Investments, she felt the tension ease away. Now, she could deal with Mr. Arvind Head-In-His-Ass Thompson.

She arrived back late but didn't particularly care. Getting docked in pay was well worth the time she'd spent with Chad. Her face flushed as she remembered the heated session they'd just shared. If today had been any indication of what was to come, she'd have to put Chad's number on speed dial.

She entered her office to find Arvind leaning over her desk searching through the files she'd left on top of it.

"Miss Green, I don't see the Lauderdale file," he stated when she approached.

"That's because I have it."

"Oh. It would have been nice of you to leave it behind so that I could analyze it," he snapped.

"You said that we were going over it together," she reminded him.

"That may be the case however; I would have liked the opportunity to familiarize myself with it before our meeting."

"Suit yourself," she said. She wasn't about to let him frazzle her again. She reached into her briefcase, got the file and thrust it towards him. He stared at the folder, but didn't open

24

it. He took in her tousled appearance and his eyes met hers with a knowing look.

"Miss Green, I'll give you fifteen minutes to make yourself presentable for our meeting," he smirked.

"See you then," she said breezily and floated off to the ladies room.

Arvind's eyes slanted. He wasn't stupid by a long shot. He knew what that extra pep in her step meant. Earlier in the morning she wore lipstick. After lunch, she'd returned without it. She'd gone off for lunch and had gotten laid. He couldn't understand for the life of him why that thought bothered him so much. Miss Green was a grown ass woman; she could do whatever she wanted. It had nothing to do with him.

But had she really done that?

His brow was furrowed in concentration when Dominique walked into his office ten minutes later.

"I'm ready," she stated sweetly.

"Have a seat," he offered, glancing up from the Lauderdale file. She'd tidied herself up, replaced her lipstick and fixed her hair. He couldn't let thoughts of her lying up under some man enter into his head. It was time to get down to business. Like he'd told himself, her personal affairs didn't concern him.

Did she smell like Coast deodorant soap?

"I've gone over the letters and requests that Mr. Lauderdale has sent to us. How did my uncle and Jack Lauderdale get along?" He

25

leaned back in his seat and waited for her answer.

"Oh, they had established a good rapport. They'd even begun golfing together on Saturdays," Dominique informed.

"Golfing?" Arvind asked incredulously. "My uncle? Humph. I've never known him to golf. That's news to me."

"Seems like you didn't really know your uncle that well," Dominique commented dryly. "He loved to play golf."

"Apparently, playing golf was up their on his list with *playing the field*. I'm sure you don't have too much to say about that, do you?"

"What are you implying, Mr. Thompson? If you're suggesting that your uncle's and my relationship was anything but professional, you'd better think twice before revealing it," she stated in warning.

Yes, it was definitely Coast that he smelled. And Coast was clearly a masculine scent.

He shook his head to clear it. "Miss Green, forgive me for that comment. I was out of line. The type of relationship you had with my uncle is none of my concern. What is my concern is that we maintain the highest level of professionalism, with senior level attention to detail to Lauderdale Capital."

"I agree," she said, exhaling and settling back down.

"Update me on them. Tell me everything that you know since you've been working so close with them over the past few months."

"I know that they are a company that has integrity. It governs every thing that they do."

"I like that," he nodded. "Go on."

"To date, the firm has an outstanding reputation and a very successful track record in all of their business dealing."

"That's great," he commented. "Mr. Jack Lauderdale, what do you know of him?"

"He's a religious man; a devout Christian. He's family oriented and an all out nice guy from what I could see."

"You ever went out with him?"

"Not personally, no. Of course, your uncle and I have held business meetings with him," she stated.

He flipped through the file that held important documentation. "I see that they're looking to establish a joint venture with us, possibly a partnership."

"That's our primary goal- to eventually go into partnership with them. Lauderdale generally seeks real estate investments requiring a minimum of $3.0 million in equity capital. They deal with the big bucks." Arvind whistled and placed his hands behind his neck.

"Pretty impressive. Well, let's establish the joint venture first. Once we see how things flow, we'll be able to decide about becoming partners with them later."

"They will definitely be a huge asset to us, especially with improving our access to financial resources," Dominique said. "Plus, with them, we could spread the costs and risks on this upcoming project."

"You're right. That's good insight on your part," he complimented. "I see you really have done your homework," he added.

"I wouldn't have it any other way. When we bring in clients that help us to make more money, I stand to gain."

"So, it's all about you, huh?" His brow lifted as he stared at her.

"Why not?" she quipped. "Even though money is the root of all evil, I can never get enough of it."

"That verse is often misquoted," he said.

"Excuse me?"

"That verse about money is often misquoted," he repeated. "The entire verse says, "For the *love* of money is money is the root of all evil." So, it's not the money that's to blame. It's the love of it."

"Well, thank you for pointing that out. And exactly where did you come up with that? It's classic," she said in sarcasm.

"It's from the Bible," he said softly.

"Oh," Dominique could only swallow down her shame. She would have known that if she hadn't fought so hard not to become like her mother. Her mother was one of those religious types that preached hell fire and brimstone type of condemnation. It had either been her way or no way, no in-betweens. Dominique had been forced to attend church every Sunday. Most Wednesdays and Fridays found her at Bible study. She'd never been allowed to lead a normal childhood. Church events had dominated most of her days.

Dominique couldn't stand being raised in such a strict environment. To this day, she didn't believe any of the Biblical principles she'd been taught. Her stepfather had been a pastor and the biggest hypocrite in the church. She'd never believe any of the words that he'd preached.

Right before her eighteenth birthday, she'd broken the chains and left home to attend FAMU on a full scholarship. While away at college she hadn't been in touch with her mother very often. Even now, she still kept a safe distance. Her lifestyle and her mother's lifestyle didn't mix.

Thinking about the strained relationship between herself and her mother caused Dominique to frown. Arvind glanced up from the file and caught her confused expression.

"Are you okay?" he asked softly.

"Oh, I'm fine," she said, recovering quickly. "I'm just tired. I can't wait to get home and soak my aching muscles."

"I'll just bet they're aching," he said under his breath. Dominique's comment had caused him to conjure up thoughts of her and her unknown lunch partner.

29

I know that's Coast. Earlier this morning she smelled like Escape.

Had she gone to lunch and had a tryst?

"Well, if you don't need me any further, I'd like to go now. I have a nail appointment at five and I don't want to be late." Her voice cut into his thoughts.

He almost blurted out that she'd been late returning from lunch, but if he did that, she'd know that he'd been watching the clock. He didn't want to start off being that kind of boss. He wanted employees who respected him. He wanted to establish a good working relationship with each and every one of his former uncle's employees. He especially wanted to develop one with Dominique. At the moment, he just didn't know exactly what kind of a relationship.

"You can go. You did come in early and I appreciate that. Thank you," he said.

"Is it fair to assume that I can come in at my regular time tomorrow morning, being that you don't drink coffee?" she added, bringing back the incident from earlier.

Her comment brought a broad smile to his face. He would love to have been a fly on the wall when he'd tossed the coffee she'd given him. Surely, the look on her face had to have been priceless?

Dominique couldn't figure out for the life of her what he found so amusing. She didn't get paid nearly enough to be the brunt of his sadistic jokes. She had to leave before she decided to get ethnic after all and tell him about himself.

"See you tomorrow, Mr. Thompson. Have a nice evening," she said through tight lips. Without waiting to hear a reply she got up and strutted out.

Chapter Three

Dominique slipped out of her heels and padded to the kitchen in her nylons. She wasn't worried about snagging them on something because they had already been ruined. She could blame that on Chad. He'd used them to tie her hands above her head. Thinking about it made her laugh out loud.

Chad was a straight up freak. Even though he was ten year younger, he didn't mind trying new things. Plus, he liked to take control. She wasn't used to being dominated, but with Chad, she really didn't mind going along with his kinky ideas. It spiced things up and kept her going back for more.

She took out some leftovers, which consisted of combination lo mien noodles from the day before to heat up. She carefully took the metal wire from the box before sticking the container in the microwave. Once she'd made the mistake of putting a container in the microwave without taking the metal piece out and ended up short-circuiting the damn thing.

While she waited for the food to heat up she looked at her freshly done manicure. She hadn't been in the mood for anything fancy, just some nail tips. One day she'd attempt to grow her own but she had a habit of biting her fingernails.

She stopped staring at her hands and checked the answering machine. For some reason she preferred to have an old fashioned answering machine instead of that voice secretary offered by the phone company. She'd tried that and had always forgotten the number to call in order to get her messages.

She frowned when she heard her mother's voice.

"Nicky, I need for you to call me. It's important."

Now, her mother rarely called her for anything. She forgot all about the Chinese food and picked up the phone.

"Mama, it's Nicky, what's wrong?" she asked as soon as her mother got on the phone.

"If l had someone else to call, I wouldn't be bothering you," she said stiffly, then, got straight to the point. "I'm going in for cataract surgery and after the surgery I'll need to recuperate for a few days. I wanted to know if I could stay there?"

"You mean with me?" Dominique gulped.

"Yes, at your place. Or either you could stay over here for a while?" Dominique immediately dismissed that idea. There would be no way she'd set foot in that religious shrine. At her mother's, you couldn't even go to the bathroom without the eyes of Jesus

33

watching. It made her skin crawl. "Nicky, are you there?"

"Yeah, I'm here Mama. You can stay with me," she finally said. "When is the surgery and are you going to need for me to pick you up?"

"It's tomorrow at two o'clock and I'll catch a taxi. Don't want to trouble you too much. You letting me stay over there is truly a blessing."

"Okay Mama, I have to go now." She wasn't in the mood for a sermon. "Do you still have that spare key that I gave you?"

"It's somewhere in my purse. But, I know I got it."

"Good. When you get here, I'll probably still be at work. So, just let yourself in and make yourself at home."

***

Dominique had spent the day pouring over figures with Arvind. They'd spent the rest of the time on the Lauderdale account. Since Brenda was still out, she'd also had to type up a few memos. When five o'clock had rolled around, she had been too glad to leave. Amazingly, Mr. Thompson had been civil the entire day.

When she stepped into her apartment, the aroma of pork chops teased her nostrils. The familiar smell caused her stomach to rumble. She hadn't had pork chops in quite a while because of her strict diet. Besides, she never could cook them like her mama. She hadn't liked the taste when she'd used Shake N Bake. It just wasn't the same.

"Hello Mama," Dominique called out.

"In the kitchen, dear." She found her mama stirring a skillet that held pork chops smothered in brown gravy.

"Should you be up?" she asked.

"I'm okay. They just told me not to life anything heavy. That's all."

"Mama, how can you see in those?" She wore dark shades that had to be thicker than Stevie Wonder's.

"I can see just fine. I have to wear these until my next appointment."

"I'm sure it's okay if you take them off inside."

"I'll do no such thing. I don't want anything causing a setback. You do want me out of your apartment in a few days, don't you?" she added.

"Calm down Mama. I was just saying. Besides, you can stay here as long as you need. You know I don't mind."

A short pause lingered then her mama sighed tiredly. "Why don't you sit down and I'll fix you a plate. You are hungry, aren't you?"

"Yes ma'am, I'm practically starving. I worked right through lunch. Did I tell you that Mr. Troutman died?" she asked, pulling out a chair and plopping down.

"He did? No, you didn't tell me." her mother exclaimed, turning from the stove. "Why you didn't call me up and tell me? At least I could have made it to the funeral. You know, his wife and I went to the same church before she married him. Then they became Lutherans." Dominique watched as her mama piled food on two plates.

"Luciferan," Dominique quipped.

"What was that?"

"Nothing, Mama. Yes, Mr. Troutman kicked the bucket. Just like that. They said it was a heart attack. You can still attend the funeral 'cause he's not in the ground yet. I'll have to find out when and where the services will be held."

"That's a shame."

"Now, his nephew is running the company."

"I didn't know he had a nephew. What type of person is he?"

"He's an as- he's anal," she said catching her slip of the tongue.

"I meant, is he a Christian?"

"Mama, I don't know. I don't go prying all into that man's personal business. Besides, I can barely stand him. Ever since Brenda's been out sick, he's had me doing my job and hers."

"You know, according to the Good Book, we are to bear one another's burdens."

"I understand Mama and I'm doing my best. It's just that Arvind-" Her words trailed

36

off. "I just can't figure him out." She told her mother about the coffee incident.

"Maybe it was just a test," Mrs. Green said, placing a plate in front of Dominique. The aroma floated into her nostrils causing her to forget all about Arvind. She dug into the pork chop and took a huge bite.

"This is scrumptious," she said. "Even though pork is the last thing my waistline needs, I'm going to enjoy every last fattening bite."

Mrs. Green looked across the table at her daughter and couldn't hold back her laughter. "Child, you are something else. If you're worried about your waistline now, just wait until you start having babies."

***

"Nicky, why don't you have any Bibles on your bookshelf?" Mrs. Green asked later. They sat in the living room watching television.

"I keep my Bible on my nightstand." But, it's not like she ever read it. She wasn't going to tell her mother that though.

"Well, it's good to have more than one version. You know they got the King James Version, the New King James Version, the New International Version. I got one called the Devotional Bible. It's easy to read and it has notes."

"That's nice Mama," she said absently flipping through the pages of Ebony magazine. She wanted to read the article they'd written about Tyler Perry. She'd loved his movie, *Diary of a Mad Black Woman,* mainly because that fine Shemar Moore played in it. She didn't think Kimberly Elise was all that cute, but that was just her opinion. It looked like she needed a new weave stylist. It was just something about her eyes that gave her a crazed look. She certainly was lucky, getting to play Shemar's love interest in that movie. What Dominique wouldn't give to be able to go a round with sexy bones. Tyler Perry wasn't half bad himself. She'd even give him a run for his money.

"You should read the book of Ruth," her mother said.

"Huh?" She glanced up from the article.

"I said, you should read the book of Ruth when you get time. It might give you an idea on how to get a husband."

Dominique tossed the Ebony magazine aside. "Mama, what is with you all of a sudden? First, you made the comment about babies, now you're talking about husbands. Are you implying that I need to get married?"

"Well, you ain't getting any younger and neither am I," her mother said. "Besides, there's something I haven't told you." Now Dominique's heart skipped a beat. She didn't like her mother's tone of voice.

"Mama, what haven't you told me?"

"I just didn't want to worry you. You know, I've always wanted to have a closer relationship with you, but now-"

38

"Mama, what is it?" Now she was beginning to get more than a little nervous.

"The doctor told me that I have high blood pressure. You know what that means," she finally said.

Dominique exhaled the breath of air she'd been holding in her lungs. Thank God she hadn't said she had cancer or something else that was fatal.

"Mama, that doesn't mean anything. It means that you're going to keep your blood pressure down."

"My mama died from a stroke. You remember that, don't you? And her mother suffered two strokes before she died. High blood pressure is serious."

"I know it's serious. That's why we're going to keep yours down," she said firmly. "Mama, I'm not ready to lose you." She felt a lump form in her throat and swallowed it down with difficulty. Her mother came over and gave her a tight hug. She wanted to stay in her mom's arms forever. That way, she'd know that she was always safe.

***

Over the next few days Dominique and her mother actually bonded. Dominique could sense that her mother had changed. She wasn't carrying on about hell all the time. She wasn't overly critical of Dominique's way of life. She didn't point the finger or accuse her of being such a sinner.

39

"You know, I've been visiting different congregations," Miss Green told her one morning over coffee.

"What? Mama, you left the Holiness Church of Christ?" That was news to her.

"Sure did. It was hard because I'd belonged to that church for over thirty years. But, I had to go."

"Why did you leave?" she asked, curious.

"Sometimes, you just have to find out things for yourself. One day, you just have to sit down and have a one-on-one conversation with God. He'll lead you in the right direction. If you're lost, He'll lead you back on the path so that you can be found. Right now, I'm at a point where I just go where He takes me. I follow in His footsteps. When I'm too weak, I let Him carry me."

"That's amazing," she said, meaning it.

"Yes it is. Nicky, you know, nobody can love you like God. And it's that same kind of love that a man and a woman are supposed to have for one another."

Chapter Four

Dominique hadn't wanted to stick around after the funeral services but her mother had insisted. She spotted Arvind among the rest of his family members and seeing him caused her heart to jolt. He looked sad and for unknown reasons that touched Dominique.

"Nicky, introduce me to your boss," her mom insisted. "Isn't he here?"

"Yes. He's right over there," she said, pointing inconspicuously.

"Well, let's walk over and offer our condolences."

"Okay," she agreed reluctantly. Funerals weren't her thing. The only reason she had attended was out of respect for Mr. Troutman. He had been a pretty decent boss. When she let herself think about it, she actually did miss him, a little.

Arvind frowned when Dominique stepped into his line of vision. She gave him a tight smile and tried to remember to behave civilly. It was, after all, his uncle's funeral.

"Mr. Thompson. This is my mother, Mrs. Geradine Green." She stepped out of his line of vision. Arvind's eyes, which seemed to have lost their luster, came to life when he looked at Mrs. Green.

"Mrs. Gerry. Is it really you?"

"Vinny. My, you have grown up. I had no idea that Mr. Troutman was your uncle. I am

41

so sorry for your loss," she said sincerely, clasping his hands in hers.

Mrs. Gerry? Vinny? Dominique took in their reunion and wondered how in the world they knew each other. She didn't have to wait long before she got an answer.

"Nicky," her mother said turning to her and smiling happily. "Vinny was in my fourth grade class. He was one of my brightest students." She beamed as she spoke.

Dominique remembered that her mother had taught private school for more than twenty years. She'd also taught in the public school system as a substitute teacher. She'd retired two years prior. She'd received many awards and certifications for being such an outstanding teacher. Her retirement party had been a huge affair. Even the mayor had made an appearance.

"Your mama was my favorite teacher. She wouldn't let me get away with any of my old tricks, although I tried." He smiled remembering. "It is so good to see you again."

"Likewise." She gave his hands a pat and released them. "God has His reasons for everything. Just remember that His grace is sufficient for you."

"Thank you Mrs. Gerry." His voice caught and he looked down at his feet.

"Stay strong. Keep the faith," Mrs. Green told him, causing him to lift his head up to stare into her face.

"I'll try," he said softly.

"You will succeed," she said with conviction. "Maybe we'll invite you over for dinner before I have to go back to my place. I'm staying with Nicky until I recuperate," she explained.

"Recuperate?" His brow furrowed in concern.

"Oh, it was cataract surgery. Nothing major. I'm doing just fine. Now I can see better than before. Almost 20/20 vision." She spotted Mrs. Troutman and excused herself. "I have to go speak to your aunt, Barbara now. You take care."

"You do the same, Mrs. Gerry." She walked off and they watched her and his aunt embrace each other.

"So, you're Mrs. Gerry's daughter," he said turning to stare at Dominique. "She always bragged about you to the class. You really made her proud," he revealed.

Dominique shifted uncomfortably. A long time had passed since she'd done anything that her mother would be proud of. She couldn't share that with Arvind, though.

"For all it's worth, I really am sorry about your uncle's death," she told him. "He was about the only friend I had in the company. I mean, he really cared – and he listened." She gave him a sad smile. "He was kind of like the father I never had," she admitted.

***

Arvind sat drumming his pen on the desktop. Dominique had left for lunch.

Brenda had returned to work and business was back to normal. His uncle's death had affected his employees, but only his immediate family had to deal with the constant grief.

He remembered the gathering back at Uncle Lenny and Aunt Barbara's house after the burial. There had been tons of food even though he hadn't felt much like eating. His mother, stepfather, and stepsister had flown in from California. Even though she'd divorced his dad and had moved on, she was still considered part of the family. He was grateful for an opportunity to visit with them before they left. He'd also gotten a chance to talk to his brother who he hadn't seen in years. Mark lived in Memphis even though he'd been born and raised in Arkansas.

His father, Uncle Lenny's brother, hadn't shown up but it hadn't surprised Arvind. Nothing could get him on an airplane. He had asked Mark about him.

"So, what's Dad up to these days?"

"Still the same old miser. Since he retired from the oil refinery, he stays cooped up in the house all the time."

"Is he still drinking?"

"I'm certain of it. I don't really go by there much. You know how he is."

"Yeah, I know," he said lowly.

"Hey, Vinny, I might need you to come visit me in Memphis," Mark said, changing the subject.

44

"Yeah?"

"Yeah. I might need you to be my best man. You know dad isn't going to do it," he added.

Arvind had slapped him on the back and congratulated him. It was about time Mark had decided to get married. He and Wilma had been together for twelve years and had five kids.

Mark and he had caught up on old times. He'd been glad that he'd gotten a chance to talk to his little brother. It didn't matter to them that they had different mothers. Mark would always be his brother.

Arvind continued to drum the pen against the desk. Something stood out in his memory and he couldn't shake it. At the church, Dominique had said that his uncle had been like a father to her. If that were the case, Lauretta would have had to make up the sexual relationship between the two. It kept agitating him and he couldn't let it rest until he'd gotten to the bottom of it.

A tap sounded on his door. His heart filled with elation but as soon as he saw Brenda, it dissipated.

"Hello Mr. Thompson," she greeted cheerfully. "I have those reports that you asked for."

"Thank you Brenda. By the way, how's your son?" he asked.

"Oh, Brendan is much better. He's back in school and functioning normal, as well. Thank you for asking." She turned to leave.

"Oh, before you go. I have another question."

"Yes?"

"I've learned that you've worked for my uncle for nine years. Miss Green just recently got promoted to Account Executive." He hesitated, wanting to pose the question the right way. "Was there something going on between the two?" he asked casually. "You know, romantically?"

Brenda appeared to be appalled that he'd even consider such a thing.

"As far as I know, your uncle loved his wife. Dominique and he attended seminars together, went to lunch together to meet with perspective clients, but it was always very professional. I certainly saw nothing wrong with their relationship."

"I don't get it," he said more to himself than to Brenda. "Why would Lauretta lie?"

"Lauretta? Tall, thin Lauretta from New Accounts?" she asked.

"Yes. Lauretta Smith."

"Oh, now I understand," she said shaking her head and tsking. "Mr. Thompson, you can't believe anything that comes out of that woman's mouth, I'm afraid. Besides, she's been peeved with Dominique ever since Dominique got promoted to supervisor of the New Accounts department. It seemed every

promotion Dominique received, the nastier the
rumors Lauretta would spread about her.
Just plain old fashioned jealousy."

Arvind shook his head. "Thank you for
clarifying that Brenda."

"No problem. I'm going to lunch now.
Dominique should be back if you need
anything," she informed.

"Thank you Brenda and enjoy your
lunch."

Arvind couldn't understand women. Why
would they try to tear each other down
because of pettiness? Obviously, he'd
prejudged Miss Green. Now he had to wipe the
slate clean and find a way to get to know the
real Dominique. The fact that she had nothing
to do with his uncle's death made things
easier.

Chapter Five

Dominique sat on the edge of the bed in the guest room, watching her mother pack a small suitcase. She almost felt sorrow in seeing her mother go. She'd really enjoyed the short visit.

Mrs. Green's eyes were adjusting well and she'd gotten the okay from her doctor to carry on as usual. Once finished, she shut and zipped the suitcase.

"Mama, you got the information that I gave you about high blood pressure, right? And the recipes?"

"Yes, they're right here." She patted a large tote that she had slung over her shoulder.

"You make sure to follow those recipes. Cut back on the salt. Stop using it altogether."

"Okay, Mama," Mrs. Green smiled.

"And we're going to walk at least twice a week, remember?"

"Yes. Six o'clock sharp." She reached for the case.

"I got that Mama," Dominique said grabbing the handle. "You should have let me drive you home instead of calling a cab."

"You know Nikki," she said softly. "I really don't want you coming home until you're ready." She stared into her daughter's face. "I don't know why you've stayed away for so many years but I'm praying that someday, you'll trust me enough to tell me."

48

Dominique's eyes clouded over. "I think your taxi is here," she said, picking up the suitcase. She hurried out the room before her mother could say anything further.

***

Dominique spotted the roses right away. A big bouquet sat in the center of her desk. The sight cheered her immediately. But, when she read the card, her delight turned to puzzlement.

"Arvind Thompson?" *What the hell?*

"Good morning Dominique," Brenda greeted as she floated by and placed something in Dominique's "In Box." "Wow, such pretty flowers." she complimented. "A secret beau?"

"Nope. More like a boa constrictor," she said with glum. "Tell me something, Brenda." She waited until she had Brenda's undivided attention.

"Yes?"

"Why would Mr. Thompson send me flowers? It's not Secretary's Day. Even if it was, you're the secretary. What's really up with this?" She stared at the flowers warily.

"I guess he just wants to cheer you up."

"I'm sure that he doesn't care."

"Maybe he feels guilty about something," Brenda suggested, shifting her gaze. She reached over to turn on a small radio that sat on Dominique's desk. Soft jazz floated on the air.

49

"Brenda, are you keeping something from me?" Dominique demanded to know.

"Well-" Brenda hesitated. She really didn't like to gossip. But, telling Dominique about Lauretta wasn't really gossiping, it was truth. "It seems that Miss Lauretta has been at it again. She's been filling Mr. Thompson's head with a bunch of garbage about you and his uncle."

"Oh my damn." She should have known something was up.

"But I set the record straight," Brenda rushed on to say. "I told him that Lauretta has been jealous of you for some time and he really shouldn't believe one word that comes out of her mouth."

"Thanks for having my back Brenda. I tell you, the way WE do each other. Why can't black people just be happy for each other?"

"In order to get ahead, some people like to pull other people down. It's like crabs in a bucket," Brenda pointed out.

"Yeah, and that crab better watch out before she gets de-clawed."

"Let go and let God," Brenda advised.

"You sound just like my mama." Dominique pursed her lips distastefully. The phone in the other room rang and Brenda hurried to answer it, ending their conversation.

Dominique sat down and stared at the roses. She still didn't know how she felt about Arvind Thompson. Only time would tell. But she had to admit the roses made her feel warm inside.

***

Dominique received a call from her mother before lunch.

"Nikki, we forgot to invite Vinny over for dinner."

"Vinny?"

"Yes, you know, your boss, Arvind. Remember, I told him that we'd invite him over for dinner? Well, it just plain slipped my mind."

"He'll be okay," Dominique stated dryly.

"Now, that's not right," she chastised. "I keep my word. I do what I say I'm going to do. So, this evening I'm cooking dinner and I want you and him to come."

"Mama. What if I have plans?"

"Do you?" There was a heavy pause. "Well?"

"No," she grudgingly admitted.

"Good." her mother exclaimed. "I'd like to invite him myself but the secretary already told me that he's in a meeting. So, you invite him, okay? Dinner will start at six."

"Mama-"

"Bye."

"But-" All she heard was a dial tone.

"This is just great." She said sourly, leaning back in her seat and exhaling.

"What's great?" Arvind's voice caused goose bumps to rise up on her flesh.
"Anything that I can help you with?" His eyes

51

met hers, making her momentarily speechless.

"Er- actually, that was my mother on the phone." She managed to finally speak. "She wanted to invite you over for dinner this evening. But, I'm sure you have better things to do," she added quickly.

"Actually, I have nothing planned. I was going to catch the end of Dr. Phil while I micro-waved a TV dinner," he said.

"Oh? Fascinating. Well, it starts at six and we're both invited."

"You want to take one car?" He suggested. "We can work up until five-thirty then leave together."

Dominique could find no way to talk herself out of going to dinner. Besides, she didn't want to disappoint her mother so she just nodded. "Thanks for the flowers," she told him. "They're lovely."

"They reminded me of someone," he said softly and their eyes locked. Dominique was the first to look away.

They had decided that Dominique would drive since she knew the way to her mother's and wouldn't have to keep giving him directions. As they headed across the parking lot towards her car who, but Lauretta Smith should they run into?

"Hey girl." Lauretta greeted in her phony manner. Dominique had the mind to tell her about herself but she didn't want Mr.

Thompson to deem her ghetto. She threw the barracuda a tight smile.

"Hi," she said flatly.

"You headed out? What you got planned for tonight?" The snake stood there grinning as she waited for Dominique's answer.

None of your fucking business. "I'm going to my mother's for dinner."

"Oh, that's nice. Hello Mr. Thompson." Her lust-filled eyes took in his tall, muscular frame. She stuck her breasts out further and gave him a bright smile.

"Hello." He didn't appreciate her lying to him. If his greeting seemed less than enthusiastic, so be it.

"You got anything special planned for tonight?" she had the nerve to ask. "I'm going to Wet Willy's for a couple of drinks. You're invited." Her eyes were hopeful.

"Thanks but I don't drink," he stated. "I'm a recovering alcoholic."

"O-oh, I didn't know that," she stuttered. "Well, okay. Anyway. You two have a good evening." She gave a little wave and hurried off. Neither of them replied. They just watched her get in her vehicle and drive away.

"I guess I'll have to tell Mama not to bring out the wine," Dominique said. "She likes to have a little after dinner."

"You don't have to do that. I don't have a drinking problem. I just want to see how fast that bat can run that through the rumor mill."

Dominique actually laughed and it was music to Arvind's ears. He realized that it was the first time he'd ever heard her laugh. He got a warm feeling inside his chest.

***

Dinner turned out to be a pleasant affair. Mrs. Green had made chicken Parmesan with angle haired pasta served with a steaming broccoli and cauliflower mix on the side. They drank tall glasses of Lipton iced tea with a slice of lemon added.

The conversation flowed smoothly. Mostly, Mrs. Green and Arvind shared stories of the antics he'd tried to pull when he was one of her students.

"I once told your mom that my brother had used my math homework to line the bottom of the hamster's cage because we'd run out of bedding," he shared. "I tried everything I could to get out of doing algebra."

"Did your brother really do that with your homework?" Dominique asked.

"No. I didn't have any hamsters," he admitted. "As a matter of fact, I didn't even have a brother. At least, not one that I knew of until later." They all laughed uproariously.

"You and that, what was his name? You two were like Siamese twins, joined at the hip."

"That was Javon Washington." He chuckled, remembering his old friend.

"Whatever became of him?"

"He made a career out of the military. Army. He's a sergeant, high up in rank. He's married with a couple of kids, now."

"When are you planning on settling down? You have anyone?" Mrs. Green threw in smoothly.

Arvind paused, took a swallow of his tea and shook his head. "No, not at the moment." He left it at that.

"Well, Nikki is single too. Seems like folk these days just don't believe in marriage. You both are in your mid-thirties. Don't you think it's about time to settle down? To start planting roots?" she asked bluntly.

"Not again," Dominique mumbled.

"Actually, Mrs. Green," Arvind said suddenly. "I agree."

Dominique, finished with her food, pushed her plate away. "Marriage is overrated," she said sourly.

"Why do you think so?" he asked.

"I mean, Mama, you didn't stay married," she said to her mother who frowned. "And look at all the marriages that end in divorce. I don't think that two people have to validate their relationship by getting some document just to prove their love."

"So, do you plan on being single the rest of your life?" Arvind questioned, looking at her with a serious expression on his face.

"I like it that way. I can come and go as I please, do as I please. I don't have to cater to anyone else's needs but my own."

"But don't you get lonely sometimes, child?" her mom asked. "Don't you want companionship? Heck, we're all grown, so I'll be blunt. Don't you want to get a lil' bit without feeling all the guilt?"

"Mama." Dominique gazed at her in shock. Her mother had never been so outspoken about such subjects. Maybe she'd have to check out that new church group she'd been hanging with.

Arvind chuckled. "Whew. It's gettin' hot in here."

"I'm serious. Nikki knows what I'm talking about. All her life she was raised up in the church. She knows all about the sins of the flesh and what separates us from God. Wouldn't it be easier not to commit fornication if you were married?"

"Mom, that sounds all good. But in the real world, it's not that easy. I mean, where would I find a man worth marrying? I don't see many prospects around this city. Most of the brothers I run across are so lame. They're looking for a woman to take care of them. I refuse to settle down with a man who makes less money than I do."

"That's a bit shallow, Nikki," Mrs. Green said in disappointment. "Since when does the amount of money you make determine your self-worth?"

Dominique didn't have an answer. She shifted uncomfortably because she felt

Arvind's eyes boring into her. Did he think that she was superficial?

Thankfully her cell phone rang, breaking the tension.

"Hello?" she answered. It was Chad. He wanted to know what she had planned for later that night.

"Nothing. I'm free," she said lowly.

"Well, pencil me in," he said in sexy undertones. "Is ten too late?"

"Not at all. I'll see you then."

"Wear somethin' sexy as hell wit' ya ass hangin' out."

"Red or black?" she asked.

"Red."

"Okay. See you at ten."

"See ya."

She disconnected, smiling. Her smile froze when she looked up into Arvind's set face. Her mother had cleared the table and stood at the sink. She couldn't hear them with her back turned.

"Midnight rendezvous?" he quipped sarcastically.

"Is it your business?"

"Aren't you a bit old to be accepting booty calls?"

"It wasn't a booty call," she answered flippantly. "Booty calls come in the middle of the night when you're already asleep. You know, like around two or three."

"I wouldn't know," he drawled. He finished off the last of his drink, capturing an ice cube between his teeth. He slurped it into his mouth then licked his lips.

If she didn't know any better, she'd think he was teasing her. Was he or could it be her hormones overreacting? It had been a little over a week since she'd last hooked up with Chad.

"Mama, thanks for dinner. We have to get going."

"Oh, you're not going to stay and have a glass of wine?"

"I'd like to stay," Arvind intercepted. "Unless, of course, you're in a hurry?" he asked Dominique with a raised brow.

"No, I'm not in a hurry. I was just thinking about your car. We left it in the parking lot and you never know what could happen. Especially with the type of security that we have." She fished for an excuse and Arvind knew it so he called her on it.

"Marcus is doing an excellent job with securing the facility. Besides, I park under the garage. The cameras are rolling," he pointed out. "So, wine or not?"

"Sure," she finally relented. "I'll get the glasses."

***

Driving back towards Troutman Mutual Funds & Investments, Dominique felt a bit light-headed. She didn't know whether to attribute it to the wine she'd consumed or to the intoxicating man sitting next to her on the passenger's side.

58

"So, Dominique, tell me a little something about yourself," he surprised her by asking.

"Er- well, there's nothing much to tell."

"Come on. Tell me what makes Miss Dominique Green tick. Let me into your world."

She glanced at him, taking her eyes off the road for a second. He seemed to be genuinely interested. "Okay. I tried to warn you. I hope my dull autobiography doesn't put you to sleep. Let's see," she began. "I was born and raised here in Tampa. I basically didn't get to do anything except go to church."

"What high school did you attend?"

"Hillsborough High. Graduated in '92. Then it was off to FAMU."

"The "Rattlers."

"Yep. For the first time in my life, I got a chance to live. I mean I was like a caged bird set free."

"Lots of wild parties, drinking, smoking weed?"

"Yes to the parties and drinking. I've never tried marijuana though. You?"

Arvind chuckled. "I'll never tell."

"You want the 411 on me, what's up with you? Where are you from?"

"I was born in a small, rural town in Arkansas. My family pretty much lived and worked the farms until we moved to St. Petersburg in 1978."

"So, you're a country boy, huh?"

"Southern gentlemen."

"Are your parents still together?"

He shook his head. "Naw. That's why we moved. Had to leave ole Dad behind." He paused and looked wistful. "He was an alcoholic and he was abusive towards my mother," he admitted, frowning.

Dominique thought his change in disposition was brought on because of the subject. But, he had other reasons. His mother had been a woman of low moral character, somewhat similar to Dominique. He knew that she'd cheated on his father. He kept that to himself though.

"Oh, I'm sorry to hear that," she said softly. They had arrived at Troutman's Mutual Fund & Investments and she brought the car to a stop next to his Lexus.

"Oh, well," he sighed. "Life goes on, right?"

"I imagine so," she said for a lack of a better answer.

He put his hand on the door handle but hesitated to pull it back. "Did you and my uncle have something sexual going on?" he blurted out.

She stared directly in his eyes. "No," she answered truthfully. "Like I told you, your uncle was like the father I never had."

"At dinner, I thought you mentioned something about your mother being married."

"It wasn't to my father and it didn't last long." She didn't want to dampen her spirits by thinking about the past.

"What the fu-." Arvind exclaimed and she snapped out of her reverie.

"What?"

"Look." He pointed up to the glass elevator connected to the building. Two people were going at it, oblivious, like there was no tomorrow. The man had the woman's skirt up and her ass pressed to the glass. Every time he slammed into her, her ass would jiggle. "Man, I tell you, white folk." He laughed, shaking his head in disbelief.

"You think black folk don't get freaky like that?" Dominique asked.

"You ever got freaky in an elevator?" He gave her a mischievous smile.

"No, but I would never rule it out," she answered.

"Are you an exhibitionist like those two?" He asked, looking up as the elevator continued upward. By that time, the man had bent the woman over and was fucking her doggy style. "I guess they're going to the top floor."

"No. I'm discreet. I don't like my business out in the streets. Everybody gossips about me enough as it is," she added.

"Just rumors. Are you admitting that it bothers you? Underneath the tough exterior is there a soft, pliable woman?"

"I wouldn't use the word pliable." Her lips twisted up in the corners in a smile.

"What word would you use to describe yourself?"

Damaged. Flawed. Imperfect. Insignificant. She thought. But, she didn't speak any of the words aloud. Stillness impregnated the air. "Survivor," she finally said.

He stared at her profile because for some reason she wouldn't look at him. "Well, Miss Survivor, I think I've taken up enough of your time. I really can say that it's been enjoyable."

"Thank you."

"No, thank you and thank your mother for me again. Dinner was delicious. Miss Gerry is something else." He opened the door to get out. "Have a good night and I'll see your tomorrow."

"See you."

After he'd gotten into his car, she drove off. As the soft tunes of India Arie floated from the car's stereo system, she replayed the moments that she'd spent with Arvind Thompson. He'd opened up a little and had revealed something personal about his childhood. She found herself wanting to know more but she had to shake it off. Besides the fact that he was her boss, he'd never want to be involved with someone like her.

She'd only told him about a small portion of her life. The rest, she wasn't proud to discuss. Once she'd made it to Tallahassee she'd gotten buck ass wild. She'd gone from one man to the next, seeking something. Yet, she'd never found it. And still hadn't. There would be no sense in trying to find it in Arvind. She could just give that idea up.

62

She pulled up in front of her place and got a nice surprise. Chad was waiting for her because she saw his black Honda with the limo-tinted windows. When she got out, he cracked his door. Smoke floated out and the scent of marijuana drifted on the air.

"You're early," she commented.

"You go 'head and get ya self ready. I'll be there in a few minutes," he told her. "I gotta get my head right."

"Well, as long as your other "head" is right, I don't mind you smoking inside," she told him.

"You sure?"

"Come on." He got out, locked his car and followed her. Once inside the apartment she offered him a seat. "Would you like something to drink?"

"I'm good. I got some Grey Goose and OJ."

"Grey Goose, huh?"

"Yeah, that Goose keep me harder than a rock."

"Well, I hope you brought enough because tonight, you just don't know how bad I want to ride your dick. And as horny as I am, I'll ride it all night long."

For a second, Chad looked at her in shock. Then he laughed. "That's what I'm talkin' 'bout. I like that shit. A woman who ain't scared to talk dirty and tell a brotha what she want and what she gone do. Hurry up and get ready befo' I pop."

"When you finish smoking your blunt, why don't you come scrub my back?" she suggested and strutted off.

"Da-yum."

***

Dominique took her time lathering her entire body with Caress. She loved the way the soap foamed up and left her body feeling soft, silky and smooth. The little bubbles tickled her skin as she softly worked the loufa sponge. She had her eyes closed, enjoying the warmth of the water as it trickled down upon her. She thought about the couple doing it in the glass elevator and it turned her on. She reached down and touched herself.

Chad entered and stood watching her through the glass-enclosed shower. When she lowered the sponge between her thighs he spoke.

"Why don't you let me do that?"

Dominique's eyes opened and she gave him a sexy grin.

"Come on in," she invited. Having him in the shower with her would be even better than fantasizing about the horny couple.

Chad wasted no time getting out of his G-Unit wear. When he slipped off his boxers, Dominique felt herself pulsating just from seeing the size of him. His stiff manhood was rock hard and saluting. She licked her lips in anticipation.

He climbed in and she moved to the side, allowing the water to fall on him. She began to lather his body with the soapy sponge. Chad was tall and gorgeous with golden bronze skin. He had a pretty boy, thuggish look about him that appealed to her. His soft brown eyes had laugh lines, showing that at one point in time he hadn't always been so tough. He had baby soft, wavy hair that he kept cut low and faded.

"So, you been thinkin' 'bout me?" he asked.

"All week."

"Why I had to call you then?"

"Because, I don't make it a habit chasing after men who have women," she pointed out.

"That's my baby mama," he explained.

"What's the difference? She's got you on lock down."

"That's out. I jus' be busy. You know what I be doin'." He stared into her eyes. "Anyway, you ain't got to worry 'bout my baby mama no mo'. We broke up."

"Really?" She wasn't about hearing his confessions. Besides, men lied all the time about their status. However, what Chad revealed next had her full attention.

"Yeah. I got tired of her puttin' her hands on me."

"What? She hit you?" she asked, surprised.

"Hell yea. All the time. She go into these fits and start accusin' me of all types of shit. Then she attack me and shit. I jus' push her off me and leave the house. 'Cause if I put my hands on her, I'm goin' to jail. See this shit?" He turned towards the light. Dominique could see scratches under his neck and on his chest.

"Gosh, Chad. I'm sorry. No one should have to put up with that type of behavior. Come here." She pulled him close, suddenly feeling overwhelmed with compassion for him. Here before her was a man who deserved to be treated like a king but all he got was mistreatment. She stood on her tiptoes and kissed him gently on the lips.

"Hey, watch that. You know how I feel 'bout kissin'," he said. Since they'd met, Dominique had discovered that Chad didn't like to kiss. Well, she did. She felt that kissing was an important part of foreplay. It got her juices flowing. If a man could really kiss her the correct way, she could even catch an orgasm.

Instead of complying, Dominique slid her tongue into his mouth, holding the sides of his face as she did so. At first, Chad held back but she continued to slide her tongue in and out of his mouth. She licked around his lips and sucked on his bottom lip, pulling it into her mouth.

"Shit. What the fuck you doin'? That shit's turnin' me on." She could feel his hardness pressed against her stomach. She reached down and groped him gently with her soft hands. She stroked him and massaged his balls, staring into his eyes.

66

"Relax," she coaxed. "Just let go of all the pressures." She slid down until the head of his dick was at eye level. Chad had thirteen inches of pure magnificent steel. It was the prettiest dick she'd seen so far. The shaft was long and straight without too many veins. The head was fat and spear shaped. Just like his skin coloring it was golden bronze, slightly darker in hue.

"Go 'head baby. Stick that big dick in ya mouth." Dominique liked when he talked dirty. It brought out the freak in her. Only too glad to comply, she took the head between her lips and began to bob back and forth. Then she rolled her tongue around it, making sure to get it moist. She alternated between bobbing and licking. Finally, she deep throated him while she played with his nut sack.

"Da-yum. That shit feels good. Suck that dick. You like how that dick taste don't you? Deep-throat my shit freak."

His nasty words were making her pussy throb. She wanted to feel him inside her. She wanted to come. She reached down and began to stroke her clit. "Touch on that monkey. Play wit' it. Stick two fingers in it." he instructed.

She did. He watched her as she masturbated and came all over her fingers. His hot jism shot forward and she pulled back, letting it hit her breasts.

They showered and rinsed off. The session had just begun. Dominique enjoyed hooking up with Chad because the man kept going like the Energizer Bunny.

As she toweled herself dry, Chad reached in his pants pocket for a Magnum. He was still dripping water but he was back on hard.

"I can't wait for the bedroom, I wanna fuck you now." He ripped the package open and slid the latex on his shaft. "Come on and bend that ass over this toilet."

When she did, he slid up in her a little at a time. He was working with thirteen inches so it took a second for her to accommodate him. But once her juices began flowing, it was on. He slammed into her as she threw her ass back at him. She pulled the seat of the toilet down and kneeled on it. She tooted her ass up allowing him full access to her pussy. She wanted his entire dick inside her, every fucking inch.

"Damn. I'm gonna come." she moaned. "I'm gonna come.

"Come all over this dick baby." He slapped her on the ass cheek. The pain mixed with pleasure sent chills coursing through her body. She loved being spanked and it wasn't often that she ran into men who liked to accommodate her.

Wack. He hit her again. Wack. Wack. The sound of him spanking her butt cheeks took her to higher heights. With every lick, he'd palm her ass cheek and caress it. He alternated from the right to the left.

"Ohhhhhhhh. Chad." She could feel the muscles or her pussy vibrate. "I'm coming. I'm coming. Shit. I'm com-ing.." She screamed, grabbing the top of the toilet. She held on as the spasms washed over her. "Oh shit." Her eyes were closed tight and she felt a rush go to her head.

Chad lifted her up and placed her on the plush throw rug. He pushed her legs up to her shoulders and plunged into her soaking pussy. He moved in and out like a locomotive. He pounded into her until he erupted like a volcano.

"Shit." he exclaimed as he released his load. He actually leaned close and kissed Dominique without her initiating it.

***

Chad didn't seem to be in any hurry to leave. Usually, they'd do their thing and he'd be gone like the wind. Tonight, he lounged around and fixed another drink and rolled another blunt, leaning back to smoke it.

"Hit this," he offered.

"I'll pass."

"This is the chronic. This shit will make yo' ass horny as hell."

"Um? Horny, huh?"

"Shit yeah."

"Okay. I'll try it." He handed the blunt to her. "So, what do I do, just puff on it, right?"

He chuckled. "Suck it like you suckin' a dick."

Dominique inhaled and immediately broke into a coughing fit. "Ugg. You can have this shit." She passed it back to him. "Whew." She patted her chest. Chad gave her his drink.

"Drink some of this." She took a gulp and swallowed. Immediately, her throat began to burn.

"Damn. I thought you said you had some chaser?"

"I did. It's all gone. So I'm drinkin' it straight."

"I can't drink anymore of that. What are you trying to do, kill me?"

"Nope. Jus' tryin' to help you relax. I'ma be here all night. Think you can handle this-" he groped himself for emphasis, "-all night?"

"Look, I don't want you getting into any trouble because of me. You sure you can be out all night?"

Chad frowned. "I'ma grown motherfucking man. I can do whatever I feel like doin'." He took another hit off the joint. "Besides, I'm tellin' you, it's over between me and her. I'm jus' sick of not bein' happy. I mean, me and her, we argue every day. Six years of the same old shit." He shook his head and looked at Dominique. "If it wasn't for my daughter, I would have been gone."

"I feel you." Once again, the subject matter had turned deep. Dominique didn't like that so she changed the subject. "Hey, you want something to eat?"

"I guess I could eat a lil somethin'," he said. She began to get up but he grabbed her hand and pulled her towards him. "But I'm not talkin' 'bout food."

Chapter Six

Dominique couldn't understand for the life of her why her head felt like cotton. She tried to move but her joints ached so badly that she wanted to stay still. But, she had to get up because it was Thursday and she'd promised her mother that they'd go walking. She mentally shook herself awake and finally managed to crack open one eye.

Chad's arms were wrapped around her waist so when she moved he stirred. His sleep-filled eyes stared into hers.

"Where you goin'?" he mumbled groggily.

"I have to take a shower. I'm supposed to go walking with my mama this morning," she whispered.

"What time is it?"

"It's five thirty."

"Hell to the naw." He buried his face into a pillow.

"You go back to sleep. I'll wake you up when I get back."

Dominique hopped on Interstate I-75 and took the 22 Avenue South Exit. Her mother lived off 37th Street and 23rd Avenue. It took her less then ten minutes to get there.

She didn't have to wait long because her mother was ready. Mrs. Green got in on the passenger's side. She was decked out in a comfortable jogging suit and Nike running shoes.

"Good morning." she greeted.

"Good morning Mama. Don't you look cute," she remarked, looking her mother over. Mrs. Green did the same to her.

"Nikki, you look kinda tired," she said. "If this is too much for you, you don't have to do it."

"Mama, it's not too much." She waved her off. "I just had a late night, that's all. Besides, this is really important. So, what did you have for breakfast? Hopefully, not that greasy bacon that you cook every morning."

"Nope, I had oatmeal, milk and some sliced pears."

"You didn't put a lot of butter in the oatmeal, did you?"

"No ma'am, I did not. Now Nikki, who's the mama?" She chuckled. "Child, I am going to do everything I can to keep my blood pressure down. I appreciate your concern though."

"I want you to maintain a healthy diet, Mama. I'm counting on you to be around a lot more years." Her mother reached over and gave her hand a squeeze.

"I'm not going nowhere until it's my time. It's in God's hands. Besides, I have to see you walk down the aisle."

"Shush. There you go with this marriage junk again." she groaned.

"Well, you are not getting any younger Nicky."

***

They went to Lake Vista Park. Even though it was early the park had quite a few people in it. Some jogged, ran, or walked. A few even skated.

After stretching to warm up the two took off down the fitness trail power walking. It wasn't long before Dominique could feel the soreness in her muscles. Chad had really worked her over the night before.

She felt flushed just remembering.

After the comment he'd made about eating, Chad had shown her that he was a man who said what he meant and meant what he said. He'd pulled her towards him and had kissed her dead in the center of her rosebud lips: the ones beneath her waistline. He'd planted deep, sloppy kisses, drawing in her essence, sucking on her nectar. He'd proceeded to suck on her clit, letting his tongue circle around and around, teasing it. Then he'd drawn it into his hot, wet mouth. He'd licked and twirled his tongue around her sensual knob. Then he'd stiffened his tongue and inserted it inside the opening of her.

Dominique's knees trembled and almost buckled. She held his head, pulling him into her as the waves washed over her. She felt an overwhelming sensation as she hit an intense orgasm. But Chad didn't stop. He blew gently on her button and inserted two fingers inside her wetness.

UNCROSSING HER LEGS

"Oh." she'd moaned shamelessly as his hot mouth sucked while his fingers slid into her. He worked his members in and out of her until she ruptured. Her juices spilled over like a waterfall, and he greedily slurped them up.

Dominique pushed Chad back onto the couch. She expertly put the condom on him and straddled his dick. She felt wild and uninhibited and knew the drag she'd taken from the weed had probably kicked in. She lowered her pussy down onto his stiff shaft. Once she could feel the length of him she bounced up and down then moved her hips in a circular motion. Chad was going crazy, moaning like a little bitch. That turned her on even further. She loved being in control and having such power.

"Throw that shit, baby. Throw it. Bounce on this dick." He grabbed her ass cheeks and squeezed them. She worked his dick like a stripper worked a pole. She continued to fuck him wildly, massaging his dick with the walls of her pussy. Her hot muffin sucked him in then spit him back out, only to do it again. She increased the pace, showing off her skills. From Chad's reaction, he was near the breaking point. She clasped her vaginal muscles as tightly as she could and just threw her pussy at his dick. She rode him like a thoroughbred. They both exploded at the same time, moaning and groaning, the sweat dripping off their bodies.

By the time Dominique and her mother had made it around the trail, she was ready for another go at Chad. It was just what she needed to start the morning off right.

"Mama, one time around is equivalent to two miles. I think we can call it a day."

"Good." her mother breathed.

"So, how do you feel, Mama?"

"Fine. I think I'm going to like this walking together."

"Me too." They slowly made their way back towards Dominique's car.

Dominique dropped her mother off, got back on the Interstate and headed home. She thought about Chad and how she was going to wake him up.

She went inside and hurriedly took a shower. She had to have Chad again before she left for work.

He was still asleep, snoring softly. She crawled on top of him, pressing her breasts against his firm chest. In his sleep, he moaned and pulled her closer. She reached down between his thighs and grabbed his dick, which was standing at attention. She covered him with a Magnum, thankful that she kept a box of them on hand. They had used up the three he'd brought with him.

She was already hot and moist so she slid onto him easily. Chad's eyes popped opened.

"Good morning," she said.

76

"Um," was the only word he could manager. Once again she'd taken his breath away and left him speechless.

Of course Dominique stepped into the office with vigor that morning. She felt rejuvenated from her excursion with Chad.

"Good morning Dominique," Brenda greeted.

"Yes, it definitely is," she sang.

"Would you like for me to get the coffee pot going?"

"Not this morning Brenda. I'm cutting back on caffeine," she said cheerfully.

"Well, what has you all flushed thing morning?" Brenda gave her a knowing look. "A new man or did you get a raise?"

"Neither. I just went walking this morning with my mother," she answered. Brenda was cool and she'd known her for years. However, Dominique knew that your business couldn't get out there in the streets unless you put it there yourself. Her involvement with Chad or anyone else for that matter would be news to only her.

"Good morning ladies." Arvind Thompson's voice sliced through the quietness of the morning. He stood in the doorway of her office, looking debonair as usual in his trendy business suit. He had his dreads pulled back away from his face. Somehow the look gave him an alluring appeal.

"Good morning Mr. Thompson," Brenda answered.

"Morning," Dominique managed. For some reason, seeing Arvind always put her on edge. Even though they'd spent time opening up to each other a bit, she still felt hesitant to let her guard down in front of him. There was just something about him that she couldn't quite put a finger on.

"I have some good news," he informed, his eyes shining with excitement. Both women looked at him expectantly. "I received a message from Jack Lauderdale. They're looking over the contract and if we have all our T's crossed and I's dotted, we'll be forming a joint venture with them as soon as the ink dries on the page."

"That's wonderful news." Brenda mused. "Well, since you're not drinking any coffee, instead of making a great big pot, I'll just grab a Pepsi from the vending machine," she told Dominique. "I have to have something to pep me up in the morning."

"Brenda, I'd think that having a seven-year-old would ensure that," Arvind commented, smiling.

"Having a child does have its benefits, but pepping me up in the morning is not one of those. It takes caffeine to do that." She left the two of them to go in pursuit of her addiction.

"So, how was your night?" Arvind inquired. His eyes boring into hers had such a look in them that she blushed.

UNCROSSING HER LEGS

"It was....er...uneventful," she lied.

"I hope you didn't tell your date that. Judging by that passion mark on your neck, he might have thought he was something to call home about."

Dominique gasped, quickly covering her throat with both hands. She knew that Chad had gotten a little carried away, but never had she suspected that he'd left any marks. Damn! Before she could think of any type of a response, Arvind walked off.

Chapter Seven

Dominique figured she'd grab something from the cafeteria that afternoon since she and Chad wasn't hooking up. After such a long night of being tossed, turned, licked, nipped, bit, sucked and fucked, she needed a slight reprieve. She could let her pussycat marinate for a while. Just because Chad had suddenly become single didn't mean shit. She wasn't about to make herself readily available to him or try to be tied down by him either.

Yeah, she'd fucked the shit out of him because he had the ability to make her have back-to-back orgasms. She wouldn't allow him to get any wrong ideas about them becoming a couple. They were unequally yoked and it would never do. She would certainly enjoy the sexual benefits she received for as long as they lasted.

As she headed for the cafeteria on the fifth floor, Lauretta got on the elevator.

"Hey girl. How you doin'?" she greeted.

Ugg. I can't stand this moose. "I'm doing just fine. How about yourself?" *As if she really gave a shit.*

"Honey, I had such a good time at Wet Willy's last night. Me and my friend had a blast." Dominique knew there weren't too many women of color at Troutman Investments, but that didn't mean this ghetto chick had to flock to her. They had never been and would never be "*sistahs.*" "You know they have Karaoke night, right?"

"No, I had no idea." *Like she really gave a flying fuck.* She couldn't understand why the phony bitch was trying to pretend that they were all cool. She felt that it was about time to put her in check. She curled her lips and glared at the other woman.

"Lauretta I really don't know you, but I've heard the bullshit that you've been spreading around about me," she said. Lauretta's mouth opened like a fish then closed. Dominique continued. "I don't take too kindly to bitches gossiping about me for no apparent reason. Now you're all up in my face, cheesing it up like we're the best of friends and we aren't." She put it bluntly seeing no reason to mince her words.

"Er- uh, I don't know what you're talkin' about," Lauretta denied, avoiding Dominique's gaze. She inched back into a far corner of the elevator in case Dominique decided to take a swing at her.

"Maybe it was a misunderstanding or a misinterpretation, but you apparently misconstrued my relationship with Mr. Troutman. I did not ever fuck that man. He was like a father to me. Will you be so kind as to stop lying to everybody by saying that I did?" she stated rather than asked.

Lauretta tried to play the dumb role at first then thought better of it. She would be woman enough to admit that she'd done

81

something wrong. "I just assumed that since there are not too many of US in high positions here, that you had to have done something to get there," she said truthfully. "I may have exaggerated the *what.*"

Dominique stared at her with a look that said, *Bitch, I ought to slap you.* She took a deep breath and exhaled. Obviously, Lauretta was one of those clueless, bobble-headed broads. There were some black women out there, had they been born Caucasian, they'd be blonde. Lauretta fit that mode. You can't be mad at somebody's ignorance. Dominique decided to just let it go. "You know what, Lauretta," she finally said. "I did do something, I worked my ass off. I went to college. Since I dedicated four years of my life to getting that bachelor's degree, I'll be damned it I'm not going to put it to use."

Lauretta had the nerve to look ashamed. She finally sucked air through her teeth and twisted her lips, sucking down her pride. "I was out of line. Shit, I might as well tell the damn truth, I'm fuckin' jealous. Hell yeah, I said it. You have everything. You drive a fancy car, you got a big title behind your name and you got these white men around her droolin' all over themselves for you. Shit, I'm jus' hatin' because I'm broke and can hardly pay my rent. Hell, I wish a man would toss my ass some change. But you," she looked her up and down without contempt. "You just get it handed to you. You got everything," she ended. "And I can tell that Arvind Thompson wants to hook up wit' you, too."

Dominique laughed. She had to give Lauretta her props. She had spilled it all and had been straight up. She understood how some people's perceptions of others could get twisted. She decided to give Lauretta a break. There really weren't too many of THEM at Troutman Mutual Funds & Investments. She'd rather have Lauretta building her up instead of tearing her down and vice versa.

"Girl, I ain't got nothing that you can't get yourself," she told her as the elevator stopped. "You just have to want it badly enough."

"I want to get the fuck out of New Accounts. I've been there for almost three years and I can't get transferred to another department. It sucks. I want to do something else."

"Well, what do you want to do?"

"I'd like to work on the phones, believe it or not." She chuckled. "Hell, I talk all the time anyway, might as well get paid for it."

"You know what, there's a position available in Operations. I know the manager. I'll see what I can do."

"You will?" Lauretta's eyes got as big as saucers.

"Yes. The problem with people today is that when they get ahead, they forget about other people. I'd like to be able to say that I'm not that type of person. Don't get me wrong: I am strong, determined, stubborn, dominating, and opinionated- to name a few. I don't take too much shit off of anyone, but I'm not above helping someone else out," she said in all sincerity.

Lauretta's face and whole demeanor changed. "Thank you. I really appreciate it."

"No problem."

They both headed toward the cafeteria. "You eatin' lunch in the cafeteria today? You mind if I sit wit' you?"

"Not at all."

She knew how it felt to sit all alone and feel isolated. For many years, that's how she'd felt until she'd taken an initiative.

As they walked over to grab trays and stand in the line, Dominique let her mind drift. Like she'd explained to Lauretta, she hadn't gone to college and obtained her bachelor degree in marketing for nothing. She hadn't busted her ass for four years to be working in nobody's mailroom. Just because her skin had a darker shade didn't mean she wasn't just as good, if not better than her white counterparts.

Well, she might have cheated a little bit, but her education, training and experience had gotten her further than her one sexual conquest. That had been nothing. It had just paved the way, enabling her to put her foot in the door. Ever since, she'd continued to high step her way to the top, letting nothing deter her.

UNCROSSING HER LEGS

Fuck what they thought. One bad decision on her part didn't make her a bad person. Besides, David hadn't been anyone important. She'd used him to get to the important people. Once she had established a good rapport with most of the VIPs, she'd been on her way. David had gotten left in the dust.

From time to time, their paths would cross and David would throw her that sad puppy dog look. He'd hint as to how much he missed being with her. She wasn't buying it though. David fucked just about everything in a dress, skirt or Capri pants. He'd been deemed, "The Italian Stallion." Where they'd come up with that, she had no idea. A stallion he was not.

She had to give it to him though; he was sexy. He was handsome, stunningly so. Tall and muscular, he resembled one of those Chippendale dancers. The looks department wasn't where he lacked. He was just a dead fuck; a two-minute man. That is, if he could get it up to last *that* long.

Speaking of the devil. As she and Lauretta sat down at one of the empty tables, David approached. To Dominique's dismay, Arvind Thompson was with him. She felt the heat rush to her face from his earlier comment. She felt like a teenager trying to hide a hickey from her mom.

After he'd left her office she'd pulled out her makeup kit and had covered it. Thank God *Mary Kay Cosmetics* could work wonders.

"Hello beautiful ladies," David flirted. "Do you two mind if we join you?" He looked mouth-watering, of course. All Dominique had to do to get her hormones in check was remember the word: pre-ejaculation. Lauretta, on the other hand was practically slobbering out the mouth. Dominique made a mental note to warn her later so that she wouldn't get disappointed. The way the two were ogling each other led her to believe they'd attempt to hook up soon.

"Of course not," Lauretta purred. She made it obvious that the seat next to her was for David. He smiled and sat down. That left the seat by Dominique vacant for Arvind.

"How's it going?" he asked.

"Fine."

"I see you're eating healthy," he remarked, eyeing her Chef salad.

"Yeah. I'm doing it because of mama. She found out that she has high blood pressure, so now she'd changing her diet and eating habits. I figured I'd do the same."

"Good choice." He had a tuna melt. Dominique didn't care for tuna and she definitely didn't like cheese all over it. Staring at his food, made her wonder if Arvind could cook. She conjured up pictures of him in the kitchen wearing a chef's apron.

"What?" He caught her staring and called her on it.

"Nothing. I was just deep in thought."

"I bet." He took a bite of his sandwich and just stared at her while he chewed. She shifted uncomfortably, spearing a tomato and lifting it to her mouth.

"Anybody watch that show called *House*?" Lauretta blurted out.

"No," Dominique answered, glad for the distraction. "I don't really watch much television. In my spare time I read, mostly."

"I tried to watch it but could never get into it. That character that plays Dr. House is such an asshole," David said. "I just couldn't get past his pompous attitude."

"That's why I like the show. He is a real trip."

"I used to watch it but with my schedule being so busy since my uncle died, I just have too much on my plate. Watching TV has become a thing of the past," Arvind shared. "Trying to handle two businesses is draining."

"Two businesses? What do you mean?" David asked.

"I own a car detailing business. Since I've recently contracted with Bayfront Medical Center, business is booming. We're on site in their parking garage and the demand for services is constant. Right now, I have someone doing my job while I take care of things here. Of course, I take over on the weekends."

"That's got to be stressful," David offered.

"Uncle Lenny's death couldn't have happened at a most inopportune time," Arvind said. "But, a man's got to do what a man's got to do," he ended, finishing his tuna.

Dominique moved lettuce around on her plate. The salad wasn't as good as she'd thought it would be. To make matters worse, she'd topped it off with low-fat ranch dressing. She really wanted a big fat greasy cheeseburger with French fries on the side. Or a T-boned steak with a baked potato, filled with sour cream and loads of margarine. She stared enviously at Lauretta and David's plates.

"Girl, I don't know why you just wasted ya money," Lauretta pointed out. "Eatin' salads is for the birds. I know I have to have some meat." She attacked her cheeseburger with a vengeance.

"I'm a meat and potatoes man too," David chimed in, taking a big bite out of his cheeseburger.

Dominique felt her stomach growl. Why the hell did she have to be the odd one out and order a damn salad?

"I guess in order to look that good, she's willing to make sacrifices," Arvind stated. Dominique smiled sweetly though she felt like stabbing him with her fork.

***

"Hey, I got some more good news. Jack just said that he finished reading over the contract and everything looks good from his end. They're going to sign." Arvind stopped by her office to inform her later that evening.

"Well, I guess there is cause for a celebration." She said, catching on to his excitement. "But remember, you don't drink," she added.

For a second, a puzzled look crossed his face then he burst into laughter. "Oh right, I'm a recovering alcoholic. Thanks to Lauretta and her big mouth, there's already a buzz around the facility about my "drinking problem." I'm telling you, that woman is like the Yellow Pages. She's got information on everything and everybody."

"This is true. I had a talk with her and I think we understand each other better. As a matter of fact, I just spoke with William in Operations about letting her transfer to his department." Dominique began tidying up her desk, straightening files and putting them away. It was close to five o'clock.

"You did?" he asked incredulously.

"Mr. Thompson, I'm not a barracuda in real life. I just act like one around here." She gave him a mischievous smirk.

Arvind watched her, thinking of ways her could get her to let her guard down more often. Dominique wasn't making it easy for him to get to know her. He thought that the flowers would have softened her a bit however; he still didn't feel a warm reception whenever their paths crossed. He wanted to change that.

"Since you're the reason we got this major account, I owe you one. You have anything planned? If not, I'll treat you to dinner." He had to slip that in.

"Well-" Did she really want to be alone with Arvind Thompson?

"Come on. I know you're hungry. All you had was that salad at lunchtime and you picked over that."

"I'm really not up to going out in public, but thanks for the offer."

"I could cook dinner for you," he said quietly.

Dominique's brow lifted. She remembered the image she'd conjured up of him in an apron earlier. She leaned up, resting her elbows on her desk and stared at him keenly.

"What's up with you? First, you buy me roses, now you're offering to cook me dinner. What are you up to Mr. Thompson?"

He shrugged and gave her an innocent look. "I'm just trying to be a good boss."

"Since when do bosses go out of their way to please their employees? I haven't encountered too many bosses like that."

"Well, I was cut from a different fabric," he half-bragged.

"But why the sudden interest?" she pressed. "I know that Lauretta told you a bunch of lame crap about me and you found out that it wasn't true, which is why you sent the flowers. You don't have to go out of your way trying to make up for that. It's in the past."

He ignored what she said. "You want me to cook you dinner or not?"

They eyed each other for a while. Dominique could feel something simmering beneath his gaze, but she didn't know what. "Fine," she said. "I accept the invite."

"Here's my address." He handed her a business card with the address written on the back. "Is six-thirty okay?"

"Six-thirty is fine." She retrieved her purse from the bottom desk drawer. "You need for me to bring anything?"

"Just your healthy appetite," he said lightly, throwing her a heart-warming smile before he left her office.

Dominique arrived at Arvind's home located in Snell Island. The house was beautiful, with a two-car garage and an outside swimming pool. The yard and shrubbery were immaculate. She rang the doorbell and waited.

It wasn't long before Arvind came to the door. "Come on in," he invited. She noticed that the living room had a masculine touch. But she only saw a brief bit because Arvind led her out to the back patio.

She surveyed his sexy body in casual wear. So used to seeing him in a suit and tie, his laid back look was a welcomed change. He looked very relaxed and, she had to admit, human.

"Well, don't you look cute," he complimented, looking her over from head to toe. She'd donned a pair of Apple Bottom jeans that hugged her hips and accented her luscious butt. The sleeveless top she wore had the words, "Baby Girl" splashed across the front. She'd pulled her real hair back into a ponytail, added light blush to her cheeks and splashed lip-gloss on her lips.

"Thank you." She took a seat at a picnic table.

The patio was one of those enclosed ones with the screens that kept the bugs out but allowed ventilation in. It had been nicely decorated with chairs that matched the bench and potted plants had been spaced out in the corners.

Arvind had grilled some steaks and fresh vegetables on the outside George Foreman grill. He'd also made baked potatoes, a simple feast.

"So, how do you like your steak?"

"Medium-well," she stated.

"I hear you. I just don't get why some people like their meat rare. We ain't Vampires." He expertly flipped the meat over on the grill. That's when Dominique noticed that he'd put on an apron. It had, *"Don't trust me in ya kitchen, 'cause I'll fuck up the chicken."* Cheesy but cute and it made her laugh.

UNCROSSING HER LEGS

"What?" He raised his shoulders in query.

"Where did you get that corny apron?"

"I ordered it from a website called TeeShirt Hell.com. They sell all kinds or weird stuff," he told her.

"Do you need any help?" she offered.

"Naw, pretty lady, I got this. Just sit back and relax." He poured some Country Time lemonade out of a big pitcher and into two glasses filled with ice. "Here you go. You do like lemonade?"

"Love it," she answered as she accepted the glass. When their fingers brushed, she felt a tingle. He looked deeply into her eyes and they stared at each other for a moment. Dominique felt something catch in her throat.

"I think those steaks are just about ready," he said, breaking the silence. He could tell by the soft look in her eyes that she had fallen for him, somewhat. He had yet to decide what he'd do with Miss Dominique Green. Maybe he'd play with her a bit before crushing her. She did it to men all the time. What goes around comes around. Or hadn't she learned that yet?

***

"I really appreciate you going all out and cooking for me," Dominique said. Arvind put their dirty dishes in the dish washer and stored away all of the leftovers.

They sat in Arvind's living room, sipping on hot Lipton Tea, of all things. She'd never known a man who drank tea.

She noticed the large bookshelf he had that was filled with tons of books. He'd even alphabetized the titles. She was impressed.

"It was no problem. You really deserve much more than that. Don't you know that with Lauderdale's business, we will become a multi-million dollar company? We are slaying the competition." He finished his tea and set the cup back into the saucer. "If I can say one thing about my uncle Lenny, he really knew how to wheel and deal. The things that seemed impossible for others became a possibility for him. He didn't let anything stop him from becoming successful." He sat back, shaking his head. "I wish my dad had been more like him."

"I'm sorry. Is he deceased?" she asked, gently.

"No." He frowned. "But, he might as well be. He lives to drink and drinks to live. What kind of life is that?" She had no answer. She finished drinking her own tea and leaned back into the plush couch pillows. Catching her at a rare moment, with her guard completely down, Arvind wanted to make the most of it. "So, tell me about your family, Miss Green."

"Dominique," she corrected, smiling slightly. "We don't have to be all formal. We're not at work."

He smiled as well. "Alright, Dominique- you and your mother seem to have a close relationship. That's good."

UNCROSSING HER LEGS

"It hasn't always been that way," she admitted. "Actually, for the majority of my life our relationship has been strained. When I went off to college, I didn't really keep in touch."

"Oh. I guess you weren't down with being forced to go to church so much, huh?"

"It's not that. Well, that's part of the reason. Truthfully- I don't know what it is. Something happened." Suddenly she stopped speaking. Visions of the past that were so vivid flew at her, daring her to forget them. "Um- I," she cleared her throat. "Can I use your bathroom?"

"Sure. It's right down the hall to the left," he said. "Are you okay?"

"I'm fine." Once again she masked her pain. How could she tell him or anyone for that matter, about what had happened so many years ago?

In Arvind's bathroom, she splashed cold water on her face. Her hands literally shook. She looked in the mirror and forced herself to face the demons of her past.

Her stepfather had raped her. She couldn't deny that and she could no longer block out the memories. The vision she'd had in Arvind's living room had been so clear. It had been of Jesse holding her down on the bed. He'd been forcing her to perform oral sex on him while her mother had been off at some church function.

TERESA D. PATTERSON

Knowing that she couldn't stay in Arvind's bathroom forever, she patted her face and hands dry then replaced her lip gloss. She'd hold it together because that was the type of woman she was. She would hold her head up high. Even though she felt the need to cry, she'd refrain and she'd maintain. No way would she ever succumb to the emotions that would outline her as being weak. Not Dominique Green.

Chapter Eight

When Dominique got in she saw that her answering machine was lit up. She checked her messages and found that Chad had left two. That was unlike him. Chad was the type who just hung up without letting her know he'd called.

Before she could even slide into her house shoes, the shrill ring of the phone sounded.

"Hello?"

"Where the fuck you been? I been callin' you all day," Chad yelled from the other end.

"Oh, hold up one minute." Dominique had to put the brother in check. She was sure that he must have bumped his damn head. "First of all, you don't call me demanding answers. And the first words out of your mouth should not be rude words. You're about to get hung up on."

"Where you been?" He insisted, ignoring the anger in her voice.

"Tending to my own damn business." she snapped.

"I been ringin' ya phone off the damn hook. I finally left a message. I thought you'd call me back but you didn't."

"Chad, I was out."

"I tried ya cell phone. You didn't answer that either," he said accusingly.

"That's because I had it turned off," she explained.

"You tryin' to avoid me or somethin'?"

"Not at all Chad. I had things to do."

"Like what?" he demanded.

"Like-" she began to answer then caught herself. She didn't owe him any explanations. "Chad, this conversation is over." Click.

Of course he called right back but she wasn't up to playing his game so she let it ring. She figured he'd grow tired after a while. She couldn't believe he was tripping like that when she'd been seeing him all of two months. The power of the pussy.

After taking a shower Dominique settled down with a good book. She was reading Water Flows Under Doors by Keith Kareem Williams, a new author on the rise. Right in the middle of a particularly good part, she heard her doorbell chime.

What the fuck? When she peered through her keyhole, she saw Chad's face staring back at her. She debated on whether or not she should let him in. For some reason, she felt that if she didn't open the door he'd start tripping. She didn't need him disturbing her neighbors. Sighing, she turned the knob, unlocking the door.

"Why you hung up on me?"

"Because you were tripping and I don't have time for that." She opened the door and he stepped inside.

"I just wanted to see you. Is somethin' wrong wit' that?"

"No Chad, but you don't control me. It's really none of your business what I do when I'm not with you."

"Well, I'm makin' it my business. Why you got me trippin' and shit?"

"That's your prerogative." She walked towards her bedroom and he followed. She had on a black, see-through, two-piece lingerie set that she'd bought at Victoria's Secret. She knew that she looked sexy as hell in it. Chad's whistle of appreciation let her know it too.

She hopped into the bed and slide under the sheets. She picked her novel back up and began reading.

"What's up?"

"Nothing. I'm reading."

"So, I can't get some attention?"

"You weren't invited over. You took it upon yourself to just show up. You're lucky I opened the door for your ass."

"You better had opened the door. I woulda kicked that bitch down," Chad told her, sitting on the edge of the bed. "I would have thought you had another man up in here. Gettin' *my* pussy." He leaned forward and caressed Dominique between her thighs. "Um. Don't that feel good?"

"Chad." She tried to pretend that she was so interested in what she was reading, but one touch from him had ignited her fire. She felt warm and moist, like Duncan Haines.

"I better not catch nobody over here. That's real."

"Chad, you don't have any rights to me. We're just casual acquaintances," she pointed out.

"Fuck that. This shit ain't casual. I don't eat jus' anybody's pussy. And I ate the hell out yours, now didn't I?" His eyes bore into hers.

"Yes," she admitted. He'd eaten it so good that she'd wanted his tongue to take up permanent residence inside her cunt.

"So, what's casual about that? How you figure?" He continued to rub her between the legs as he spoke. He eased her panties aside and slid his thumb into her wetness. She couldn't hold back the moan that escaped her lips. He caressed her clit with his other hand. "Answer me, what's casual about this?"

"Chad, we can't have a conversation with you stroking me like that. So, do you want to talk or do you want to fuck?" she asked boldly.

"You already know."

"Well, one of us has on too many clothes."

"That shit can be changed." He stood up and his thumb slid out her pussy. She needed to replace it with the real thing.

Dominique pulled him roughly against her. She wanted to let him know that she was in charge, not him. The sooner he realized that, the better.

"Hold up, this shirt cost a few duckies, you 'bout to rip it."

"I don't give a shit." With that being said, she popped the buttons and snatched it from his body. She clawed at his belt and unbuckled it, finding it an annoyance. It was blocking her from getting to what she wanted. Once she had his pants to his knees, she reached inside his boxers and stroked his manhood. It immediately stood to attention.

"Make that snake hiss, baby." Chad encouraged.

"I'll do more than that, I'll make it shoot venom."

"Bring it."

She grabbed his dick and sucked it into her mouth like a vacuum. She toyed with the head of it, bobbing back and forth, licking and slurping until she had him hard enough to pop. She licked underneath the shaft and hummed on his balls. Then, she deep throated him, driving him wild like she knew she would. Deep throating a dick was a skill that not many had acquired.

Chad hurried to get out of his shoes and pants. "Day-um, you good. I gotta get up in that."

"Wait." Dominique held up one finger. "Turn around."

"Huh?"

"Turn around," she instructed.

101

Chad gave her a puzzled look but complied. She parted his cheeks and slid her tongue between the crevices of his ass. At first he tensed up but she continued to lick and explore his crack until he gradually relaxed. She twirled her tongue around his hole then gingerly darted it in and out. As she did that, she reached around and stroked his dick. Her moist tongue went in and out, around and around, as her warm hand went back and forth.

In and out, around and around, back and forth. In and out, around and around, back and forth until Chad groaned then bust a nut all over her fist.

"Shiiiiittt." He yelled, turning around and pushing her against the mattress. Even though he'd already climaxed, he was still rock hard. Now, he was the aggressive one. He began to sink his shaft into her without wrapping it up but Dominique halted him.

"Put on a condom." She did not play that. He wasn't about to have her hemmed up, saddled with his illegitimate child. Not to mention the fact that he might have something she couldn't get rid of. She didn't know him like that.

Chad smirked. "You gonna let me tap that shit raw one day." He held his cock with one hand and slapped it against the palm of the other. "I know you wanna feel this big, fat, long dick all up in you natural."

UNCROSSING HER LEGS

"Chad, don't kill the mood. Latex that shit up and fuck me." she commanded.

"That's right. I better. After all, we just casual," he said sarcastically.

He put on a Magnum and proceeded to fuck the shit out of her. It was as if he was trying to prove something. He tried to knock her back out and make her pussy sore as hell in the process. He didn't care whether or not she came, he just wanted to beat it up and let her know that it belonged to him. He was going to wear it out so she wouldn't even think about giving it to anybody else.

After a while, Dominique began to get a little annoyed. She'd just licked that Negro's asshole, the least he could do was make her pussy jump. He needed to chill with the fucking control issues and get busy with trying to please her.

As soon as he turned over, she scooted up his chest and put it right in his face. He might be a novice at eating at the Y but when she finished with him, he'd be a pussy connoisseur.

"Yeah, put that fat cat right in my face. I'm 'bout to make it purr." She couldn't get enough of his dirty talk. She enjoyed that shit immensely because it turned her on. She rolled her hips, grinding her mound on his lips and tongue. Just when she'd almost reached orgasm, Chad grabbed her by the waist and pulled her back down onto his dick. It damn near reached her liver and it felt good as hell. He flipped her over and now he was back on top. He began bucking like a wild bull in a rodeo, just throwing that dick. She couldn't stop from slipping into oblivion. She was contracting and pulsating while he pounded the shit out of her.

"Oh Shit. Fuck me." she screamed.

"Whose pussy is this?" he growled.

"Shit. Oooohhhh. I'm coming. I'm coming." She could feel the juices gushing out of her loins.

"Whose- fuckin'- pussy- is-this?" With each word he plowed deeper into her. "Open ya eyes and look at me." He grabbed a handful of her hair and tugged on it. "I said, whose pussy is this?"

"Yours." she lied. She didn't care. She'd tell him what he wanted to hear just to catch another mind-blowing nut like the one she had just experienced.

"That's what I thought," he said smugly as she came again.

While she writhed and squirmed in the throes of passion, he quickly slipped the condom off. He wanted to feel her, really feel her. No, he needed to.

He could immediately feel a change in the sensation but Dominique was too caught up, experiencing back-to-back orgasms, to notice anything different.

Chad was in heaven. His bare dick was cocooned in her silky, hot, dripping pussy and she had no idea. He counted how many times she came with his natural dick inside her. Six. Now he was about to shoot a major load right up in her and he wasn't trying to hold back. He was determined to get another baby mama to replace the one he'd gotten rid of. This time, he'd try for a son.

Hell, Dominique's pussy was so good, a brother was sprung. Shit, he'd ask her to be his wife, just so he could get it twenty-four seven. At least Dominique wasn't a violent trick like his baby mama. She had a lot going for her *and* she was a freak. Shit, she was the freakiest woman he'd ever encountered and that's why his ass was whipped.

Chad moaned like a li' bitch, sinking further into her moistness. "Day-um, this some good pussy. Shit. I'm'bout to skeet. Awww shiiiiit.... That's it."

Dominique didn't have many friends. She'd long since lost contact with her college buddies. The friends that she'd had in high school had either moved away or had too much drama in their lives for her to contend with.

Since their talk in the elevator, Lauretta had began being more sincere. Dominique let her guard down and began conversing with her like she'd do with a girlfriend. She found that Lauretta wasn't half bad.

They had begun meeting for lunch almost every day. Sometimes, they'd grab something from the cafeteria. Other times, they'd go off to get something. It was during one of these runs that Dominique told Lauretta about Chad.

"Girl, sounds like he might be a tickin' time bomb."

"I hope he doesn't start becoming too attached because I'll have to cut his ass loose."

"Are you sure he'll let you go? He sounds like he's been whipped by the puddy cat. Once that happens, some of these men be straight up trippin'. My friend Destiny is dealin' wit' a psycho right now."

"How so?" She pulled up to the Wendy's drive-thru behind three other cars.

"Her man has turned into a true stalker. If she go somewhere he call over there to check and make sure she's there. One day, she was doing my micro braids and didn't get finished until after two in the mornin'. Do you know this fool called my home phone askin' to speak to her?"

"That's crazy."

"I know. And he gets in his car and goes drivin' around the city lookin' for her, too."

"I don't think Chad is *that* bad. But, you never know." She pulled up to the window and placed their orders. "He has definitely began to change. Especially since her broke it off with his baby mama."

"Oh damn."

"What?"

"Let's hope he ain't tryin' to get another *baby mama.*"

"I'm not worried about that. We use protection each and every time."

"I've known men to sabotage the condom."

"Damn Lauretta, you know all kinds of trifling people. Why the fuck would a bitch do that?"

"Some people are jacked up in the membrane. Jus' be careful. Unless Chad is someone you'd like to kick it with long-termed," she added.

"It's really just a sex thing. I mean, he can make my toes curl, but I'm definitely not in love with him. Girl, he began going down on me and has learned how to eat the hell out some pussy. He does make me crave his tongue action."

"Oomph..

"But I know that I'm not in love. All I want to do is fuck him."

"Spoken like a true pussy popper. Pop that pussy on a brotha then leave his ass." She reached into the bag and pulled out a French fry. "Tell me something." She chewed on the fry. "Now, I know you didn't fuck Mr. Troutman but how about David?"

Even though she'd sworn that she wouldn't put her personal business out in the streets, hell she saw no reason to lie. "I *tried* to but he couldn't get hard enough to do much of anything with that dick of his," she admitted.

"That's a shame," Lauretta said regretfully. She grabbed another fry.

"Hey, maybe things have improved. He and I hooked up well over a year ago. Maybe he got some Viagra or something. Better yet, maybe he got a dick implant."

"I heard that those stay hard." The two roared with laughter as Dominique drove back towards Troutman Mutual Funds and Investments.

Chapter Nine

Friday rolled around. Arvind had been closed up in his office most of the morning going over statistical reports. Looking at the numbers and looking at all the people that his uncle owed money to was giving him a headache. Something just wasn't adding up. If he didn't know any better, the company was headed for a major downslide.

He only stopped to take a short break when the phone rang. His brother Mark just wanted to let him know that he and Wilma had finally decided on a wedding date. It would be June 12th, which was three weeks away.

After hanging up, Arvind put the reports away. He had a wedding to attend. He had to start making arrangements in order to fly to Memphis.

Actually, he felt good about being able to get away. It would be a short reprieve. Working all the time was beginning to burn him out. He needed a break. Going to Memphis would be a pause in the chaos that had become his life.

Maybe he'd even venture out to the country and see his father. Maybe not...

Thinking about his father never left pleasant memories. He hadn't spoken to the man in years and the last time he'd seen him was at his grandmother's funeral. Even then, the man had been standoffish, with few words to say. His own mother had died and he hadn't shed a single tear. Arvind couldn't understand him and he wasn't going to waste precious time trying to figure him out.

He needed to rent a tux and shoes. He'd have to reserve a rental for when he got there. He'd have to make traveling arrangements. What about a date?

Damn, weddings were events that you didn't want to go to alone. But, he didn't have anyone who he could stomach taking to such a family function. Well, there was Deidra, but she had children and probably wouldn't be able to get anyone to keep them over a weekend. Besides, he wasn't really feeling her. She was much too needy. She had three small children with and incarcerated father. At times he felt like he was paying child support for the absentee parent. He loved kids, but Deidra seemed to want him more for what was in his wallet than in his heart. She'd even asked him to baby sit once and that's where he'd drawn the line. He didn't have any kids, but he knew that if he did, he wouldn't entrust their care to just anyone. He wasn't a pedophile or a child sexual offender, but Deidra hadn't known that.

Nope. He shook his head. He'd definitely have to rule her out.

He could invite Veronica. She didn't have any kids but she was too rough for his liking. Sexually, she was off-the-chain. She liked to try new stuff that seemed painful. The last time they'd hooked up she'd wanted him to choke her. In the end he had complied but had gotten scared because he thought he'd rendered her unconscious. She'd sworn that she'd only been having the ultimate orgasmic experience.

Hell no. He didn't want to catch a charge behind rough sex. She was also a drama queen, and he could do without the theatrics.

For some reason, Dominique flashed across her mind. Would she go? Would she think that his inviting her was out of line? Technically, he wasn't her boss. He was only the stand-in until some replaced his uncle. He really had no ties to Troutman Mutual Funds and Investments. He was just helping out his aunt Barbara, making sure that things were in order and she didn't have to worry financially. Seemed like there was nothing that could be done about that now.

Yeah, he'd do it. He'd ask her out because he really wanted to find out what the fascination was about. All the white men wanted a piece of Dominique. David had given him the 411 on the snobbish tramp. Now he knew exactly what type of woman she was.

He could kick himself for even thinking that he might want to settle down with the likes of her. He'd been blinded for a minute. He'd thought that he'd give her the benefit of the doubt because she was Mrs. Green's daughter. He'd heard of the apple not falling far from the tree. But in the case of Dominique and her mother, the apple hadn't just fallen it had rolled hundreds of miles away.

"Let's see, how am I going to work this one?" He picked up the phone.

Dominique was sitting at her desk checking emails when her phone buzzed. Arvind's number was lit up. Her heart did a little pitter-patter as she reached for the receiver.

"Hello?"

"Miss Green, do you have a minute?"

"Sure. Do you want me to step into your office?"

"Yes, if it's no trouble."

"I'll be right there." She lowered the receiver and grabbed her purse. After doing a quick check she was pleased to find her hair in place and make-up immaculate.

She got up and walked the short distance to his office and gently tapped on the door.

"Come on in."

Arvind was staring at his computer screen with a thoughtful expression on his face.

"Are you okay?" she asked.

"Oh yeah," he answered looking up. "I was just trying to figure out who has the best packaged deals on tickets."

"Tickets?"

"Oh, plane tickets. My brother is getting married and I have to fly to Memphis."

"Wow, that's great. I usually use Expedia.com."

"What about Travelocity?"

"They're pretty much the same." She took a seat. "So, what's going on?"

"Nothing much. I just wanted to ask you a favor," he said softly.

Her brow lifted. "Such as?"

"I really don't want to go to my brother's wedding alone. Would you be interested in attending?"

Dominique's mind whirled. Wow. He was asking her to accompany him to Memphis for his brother's wedding. It completely threw her off guard.

"W-well, I er..." she stammered.

"It's not for another three weeks," he said quickly. "And it's on the weekend," he added. "June 12th."

She contemplated it for a moment. "I don't have anything planned. I think getting away is a good idea. I guess my answer is, yes. Yes, I'll go."

"Well, then it's settled. Thank you."

"No problem." Dominique got up to leave.

"Oh, Miss Green. I'll make sure to reserve separate rooms, unless you'd prefer otherwise."

The following week consisted of Dominique spending time with her mother. They continued to go walking on Tuesdays and

Thursdays. Her evenings were reserved for Chad. He made it a point to call her every day. If the sex hadn't been outstanding, she would have put a stop to it long ago. It was unlike her to let anyone manipulate so much of her time. But, she'd decided to just go with the flow. Chad had proven to be an intelligent guy beneath the thuggish appearance.

Over the weeks she'd learned a lot about Chad. It had shocked her that he'd actually gone to college. He'd nearly completed his bachelor's degree in criminology. How ironic that he'd chosen to sell drugs after such a background.

He'd confessed that he hadn't been able to meet the high expectations that his mother had set for him. He'd tried and failed. So, he'd decided to do what he wanted and nobody could deter him.

"I don't punch no time clock," he had explained to her. "I come and go when I please. I don't have to answer to no body. And I make as much money as I choose to make."

"But, doesn't it get old after while?" Dominique asked.

They were sitting in her living room watching the movie *Madea's Family Reunion.*

"I don't plan to sell drugs forever. One day soon, I'll decide to get out the game. It's gonna take somethin' worthwhile to make me wanna quit."

"What about your daughter's mother? Didn't it bother her?"

"Hell naw. Her ass always had her hand out. Had them out so much, they began to look like cups. That's why I had to hustle so hard. After she had my daughter, she didn't have to do shit. She got used to that and didn't wanna get a job. When I got locked up for a bit, she had to get off her ass and take care of business. Now, she work- but she still be lookin' at me to pay for everything."

"What did you go to jail for?" Dominique was curious. "Did you get caught with drugs on you?"

"Naw, it was for a gun charge."

"What?"

He shrugged. "I was mad. Some bustas pissed me off. So I shot at 'em."

"Oh my goodness." She gave him an incredulous look. "You didn't shoot anyone, did you?"

He chuckled. "Naw. I was jus' fuckin' wit' 'em. To this day, they got respect for a brotha, tho." He sat back and rolled his blunt. "I caught another charge drivin' wit' a concealed weapon. I was supposed to do some time behind that, but my lawyer worked that out."

"Well, I hope you've learned your lesson," Dominique remarked.

"Well, shit. I do what I have to. I can't be out in these streets without bein' strapped. Hell naw. That's how you lose ya life. I have to protect me and mine. For sho'."

Dominique couldn't see it his way. Thug life wasn't any real kind of life. What example

115

was he setting for his daughter? And what did he have to show for putting his life and freedom in danger daily? All she could see was the bling bling around his neck, wrists and in his ear. Yeah, he had the most expensive clothes and footgear. But, were material possessions really worth it?

Even with his criminal background and tarnished past, Dominique couldn't cut Chad out of her life. Once he revealed his shocking secret, her whole perception of him changed.

Sometimes, they'd snuggle together and watch TV after having sex. One particular night, Chad was extremely talkative.

"You know, I've always had a big dick."

"Really?"

"Yeah. It's been this big since I was about twelve."

"No way."

"Probably because of what happened when I was a lil jit."

Dominique noticed a change in his tone of voice and gazed at him in concern.

"What happened, Chad?" she asked softly.

"I was just a baby. I couldn't a been no more than two or three. She used to pull on my dick and make me fuck her."

She stared at him, horrified. "Who?"

"My stepfather's sister. My so-called aunt," he answered bitterly.

"Oh my God."

"I was a lil' kid. She ain't have no business doin' that shit. That shit wasn't right." He shook his head from side to side. "And my mama wouldn't listen when I tried to tell. She just wouldn't listen."

Dominique was stunned speechless. Looking at Chad, she could tell that it had affected him deeply. Her heart nearly broke when a tear slid down his cheek.

"God Chad. I am so sorry that happened to you." She wrapped her arms around him and just held him tightly. At that moment, she realized that she and Chad had a lot more in common than she'd thought.

The day came when Dominique and Arvind had to make the trip to Memphis. He'd be leaving his car at the airport so he stopped by to pick her up. Already packed and ready to go she stood by as he packed her Luis Vitton luggage into the trunk.

To her utter dismay, Chad pulled into a parking space next to them. He got out of his car, staring at Arvind with a suspicious look. Arvind slammed the hood closed and sized up the situation.

"You need a minute?" he asked Dominique.

"Sure. I'll be right there. I promise we won't miss the flight," she told him. "Inside," she snapped at Chad.

Once the door had closed, she turned to face Chad angrily. "How many times have I told you not to just show up at my place?"

117

He ignored her question and began in on her. "I see you runnin' games."

"I'm not running anything."

"Who the fuck is that dude out there waitin' for you?" he demanded to know.

"That's my boss. I have to go out of town on a business trip," she lied.

"Hell naw it ain't. Ya boss is an old motherfucker. Even I know that."

"Chad, Mr. Troutman died. That's his nephew who stepped in to take over."

"Well, why you didn't mention no business trip to me when I was here the las' time?"

"It slipped my mind. Damn Chad, I don't have to tell you every little detail of my life. We are not a couple."

"How long is this business trip su'pose to take?" he asked, ignoring what she'd said.

"It's over the weekend."

Silence filled the room momentarily. "So, you expect me to believe that you goin' outta town wit' a man for the weekend and it's jus' business?"

"Chad, I don't have time to stand here and debate with you. We have a flight to catch. We'll discuss this when I return. We have a few things that need to be straightened out anyway."

"You right about that. The first thing I'ma do is fin' out who the fuck that is." With that, he turned and walked out the front door.

"Chad." She rushed behind him. She watched in disbelief as he approached Arvind who sat waiting in the car. For a while, the two carried on a conversation and surprisingly nothing violent ensued. Chad walked up to her because she'd been standing a distance off.

"I guess I'll see you when you and ya boss get back."

"I hope you're satisfied. I can't believe you'd embarrass me like that."

"I'm jus' tryin' to be in the know. I'll be damn if I let you step all ova my fuckin' heart. If you ain't feelin' me the way I'm feelin' you, just let me know."

"Chad, this is not the time, nor place to discuss this. We'll talk when I get back. I mean it." She saw Arvind holding up his wrist and pointing to his watch. "I really have to go. I'll see you."

"Bye." Before she had time to step away, he pulled her against him and planted a firm kiss upon her lips.

"Chad-" she pushed gently at his chest. "Public displays of affection are not my style."

"Right," he said, his eyes boring into hers. "I guess I better let you go." He released her. "Oh, damn. I left my cell phone on ya couch."

Dominique didn't feel like walking the ten feet to her apartment to open the door. Besides, she'd already kept Arvind waiting long enough. She reached into her purse and pulled out a spare key. "Here. Get you phone and lock up on your way out. Leave the key on my coffee table."

"Alright," he said taking the key.

Dominique rushed to get in on the passenger's side. "I'm so sorry for that," she began apologizing immediately.

"You don't have to explain yourself to me," Arvind said stiffly. He didn't want to be involved in any relationship drama. He'd lied to the guy for Dominique's sake. He'd seen something in his face that had spoken danger. "Had I known you had a boyfriend, I wouldn't have asked you to accompany me to Memphis." It was just like a selfish bitch to not reveal that information.

"Chad is not my boyfriend," she stated. "He's just a friend."

"Yeah. A friend with benefits."

"What business is it of yours?" she snapped.

He stared at her, surprised by the tone. "None," he answered.

"Remember that and just drive." She crossed her arms and stared ahead not speaking to him all the way to the airport.

Chad picked up his phone and began to leave. Suddenly, an idea popped into his head. He went to Dominique's bedroom and over to the nightstand. Opening the drawer, he pulled out the box of condoms. He then looked on top of the bureau searching for something. When he saw the needle and thread he smiled. Taking the needle out of the spool of thread, he used it to puncture a small hole in each condom package. Satisfied, he put the condoms back where he'd found them. If it hadn't already happened, it would. He was going to get her pregnant. One way or another Dominique would belong to him.

Chapter Ten

Once they'd settled in their seats on the plane, Arvind thought it best to make amends. He didn't want to piss Dominique off or he wouldn't be able to carry out his plan. Teaching the bitch a lesson was something he felt was his duty. Since he'd been a drama major, he felt confident he could pretend to be interested in her.

"Miss Green, if you thought that I was dipping into your personal business, I apologize," he said. "If I offended you in any way, I am truly sorry."

Dominique could sense the sincerity of his words. She could hold onto her anger or let it go. It really was her choice. She chose to let it go.

"Apology accepted. And what's with this Miss Green? I thought we'd gotten to a first name basis."

"Oh my bad, Nikki," he teased, lightening the mood.

"That's more like it, Vinny."

He chuckled. "So, if you don't mind me asking, who was that guy?"

Dominique sighed. "He's someone I became intimate with months ago. Since we're both single, we just hit it off. It's nothing serious."

"I don't think he sees it that way."

"Why do you say that?" she asked. The "Remove Seatbelt" light flashed so she unbuckled hers and got comfortable. Arvind followed pursuit.

"Just call it a man's intuition. You woman have it, so we can too."

"Well, you may be right. When I get back into town, Chad and I will have a serious discussion. I'll let him know just where I stand."

"Then what?" he questioned. His eyes searched hers.

"I guess I'll cross that bridge when I get to it." They both grew silent and continued to stare at each other as their eyes spoke volumes.

"Would you care for something to drink?" The stewardess's voice interrupted their eye-to-eye combat.

"Um- sure," Arvind spoke first. "I'll have a Sprite."

"If you have Pepsi, I'll take one."

"Here you go," she said, placing their drinks in front of them. Just let me know if you need anything else." She gave them a big Colgate smile.

"Thank you," they both replied.

"I should have gotten something stronger," Arvind spoke out. "I hate planes and by the time we land, my nerves will probably be shot."

"You're afraid of flying?" she stared at him in amazement. "You?"

123

"Not the flying portion, just the plane. I don't like to be closed in." He stared around. "This may seem like a large airplane to you, but to me, it's like a small box."

After a while, Dominique could tell that he hadn't been exaggerating. Sweat beads had popped out on his forehead and he'd began gripping the armrests so tight that his knuckles were turning white.

"Are you okay?" When he didn't answer, Dominique flagged down the flight attendant and requested a shot of Hennessey. "Drink this," she said, holding the plastic cup up to his mouth. Somehow, she got him to swallow the strong liquid.

"Ugg." He coughed. "Whew. That burned my throat." He seemed to relax a little. At least he loosened his grip on the armrests.

"You feel a little better?"

He nodded. "Yeah. I guess you think I'm a wimp, huh? A grown man being so scared." Dominique said nothing. "I know I should be able to shake this fear, but I can't. I began being afraid when my dad used to beat on my mom. I'd run and hide in the closet. It used to be so dark in there it scared me. But, I wouldn't come out because I just couldn't stand to see him beating her like that."

"My God." Dominique's heart broke for him. Somehow, she could picture the scared little boy he'd been, hiding and trembling in a dark closet. She reached for his hand. "It's okay," she soothed. "We'll be landing soon."

"Just keep holding my hand. I'll be fine if you just - keep holding - my-" He drifted off to sleep as he spoke.

Dominique moved as close to him as the seats could allow and laid her head on his shoulder. So, Arvind Thompson wasn't such a hard ass after all. He'd shared such a personal part of himself with her and she didn't know the reason why. Maybe this trip would be the start of a new beginning. She knew that first impressions were usually lasting impressions. She could only imagine what Arvind thought of her. If her view of him could change, perhaps his view of her could change as well.

They arrived at the Memphis International Airport with no delays. Amazingly, their luggage arrived at the same time as they did. Arvind directed them to the Avis Car Rental located inside the airport. They got the rental car and he loaded their suitcases into the trunk.

"We'll be staying at the The Hilton Memphis on Ridgeway Center Parkway. It's about twelve miles from here. I've stayed there before. The accommodations are really nice." He shot a quick glance her way then put his eyes back on the road. "And I reserved two rooms"

She chuckled. "Thank you. Are they adjourning?"

"As a matter-of-fact they are. What you plan on doing, sneaking into my room at midnight?"

"Hardly," she said sarcastically.

He threw her a smile. "I'm sorry I lost it for a minute there on the plane. Thank you for getting me through that," he told her.

"No problem."

"I have to admit, I'm a little embarrassed about the whole thing now."

"Arvind, there's nothing to be embarrassed about. We are all human and humans are allowed to feel emotions. Just because you're a man doesn't mean you have to hold everything inside."

"I appreciate you letting me hold your hand," he told her. "Whoa. There's my exit, I almost missed it," he said, swerving into the left lane. He turned on Plough Blvd and looked for the signs to I-240. He took I-240 E. toward Nashville then turned onto Exit 15a/Poplar Ave./Germantown. He then made a left onto Ridgeway Loop Road and went under the Overpass. Turning left onto Ridgeway Center Pkwy, they saw the hotel to the left

"Nice." Dominique commented eyeing the outside swimming pool. Someone immediately came to valet park the car. Another person retrieved their luggage from the trunk.

After checking in and getting the keys from the front desk, they headed to rooms 107 and 108. By then, it was almost four o'clock in the evening. As Arvind used the plastic key to open his door, he stared at Dominique. "You sure you don't want to come over here? What goes on in room 107, stays in 107," he teased.

"I'll pass. But, I would like to go get something to eat. How about you?"

"Sure. There's a nice barbeque place about a mile off called Corky's. You want to blow your diet and go there?"

"I'm not on a diet," she told him. "I just try to eat healthy. And, from time to time, I splurge. So, in answer to your question, I'll be glad to try Corky's. It had better be good."

"It's famous. All the tourists go there."

"All the tourists are probably of the Caucasian persuasion and don't know anything about barbeque," she said wryly.

"Aw, that ain't right."

"But you know I'm telling the truth. What do white people know about pork? They just began eating it. We've been eating it for years." They laughed uproariously.

"I know I'll chow down on some chitterlings and hog maws," he admitted, still chuckling. "My mama can put her toe in some collard greens, too. That reminds me, my family can throw down in the kitchen. The reception is going to be amazing. You'll definitely gain a few pounds from all the different stuff they'll be dishing up. I just thought I'd give you a fair warning."

"I think I can handle it," she said. "That's why I exercise. So that I'll be able to eat anything I want."

"Okay. When you head back to Tampa dragging an extra set of luggage in your jeans, don't blame me."

Dominique laughed again. "I'll be right out after I unpack," she told him. "My stomach is starting to growl."

"I'll be making a call to my brother to let him know I made it into town safely. Just tap on my door and let yourself in when you're ready."

Amazingly, the food was delicious at Corky's. Dominique was really enjoying her barbeque ribs. She and Arvind had ordered a whole slab. She'd also gotten coleslaw and hush puppies. For dessert, she'd chosen some sweet potato pie and Arvind had gotten key lime pie.

"Um, these ribs are good," she told Arvind as she licked her fingers." She didn't know just how appealing she looked to him. He felt something stir in his groins.

"Yeah," he managed to say and took a large swallow of his iced tea. He had to calm down. Just because he'd finally gotten Dominique alone, didn't mean that he could just jump her bones. He couldn't understand why his intentions towards her kept alternating. One minute, he couldn't stand her. The next minute she turned him on. He reminded himself that she had someone named Chad that she was giving the goods too. He refused to come second behind any man.

"I was looking at some of the brochures in the hotel room," she said through bites of food. "I'd love to check out some of the area's attractions. That is, if you don't mind?"

"Not at all. Mark's wedding and reception isn't until tomorrow."

"I don't want to take away from time you could be spending with your family."

"I'll see plenty of them tomorrow and Sunday. Let's take this night to enjoy ourselves. What are some of the places you might want to visit? Please don't say Graceland." He rolled his eyes comically. He'd been there several times and in his opinion, it really wasn't all that.

"Oh no. I have never been a big Elvis fan. I was thinking more along the lines of Beale Street."

"Where the blues was born," he said. "Now you're talking."

"Or Mud Island River Park. Or we could go bowling at Liberty Bowl."

"B.B. King has a blues club," he informed, digging into his key lime pie. "Do you like blues?"

"I haven't listened to it much, but I'm sure I'd enjoy myself," she answered, trying her sweet potato pie. "Um." she moaned. Arvind had to brace himself once again. If he weren't

129

careful, he wouldn't be able to stand up without giving himself away.

"How about we do all of the above? We can hit up Mud Island first. After that we'll go bowling. Then, we come back to the hotel and freshen up then finish the night off at the blues club. Sound like a plan?"

"Yeah. It sounds like a plan."

"Dominique, I really want you to enjoy yourself. So, you can let your guard down. Okay?"

She looked into his eyes and nodded slowly. "Okay."

"Alrighty then. Let's do the damn thing- Memphis style." he said excitedly. Dominique couldn't help but to catch on to his enthusiasm and playful mood. She actually did find herself letting down the barriers. She just wanted to have a good time and hang with pleasant company.

They took a Swiss-made monorail, which whisked them across the harbor to Mud Island River Park. On board they got to experience a wonderful view of downtown Memphis, the Mississippi River and Mud Island River Park. It filled Dominique with excitement. She couldn't stop smiling and pointing—just like a true tourist.

After departing the monorail, they decided on what they wanted to do. They could experience the river first hand by canoeing of kayaking.

"I don't think so. My feet belong planted firmly on the ground," Arvind said. "And do you really want to risk getting that fabulous hairdo of yours wet?"

"I guess that rules out the pedal boat. Well, how about riding the bicycles? We can see downtown Memphis up close."

Arvind wore a skeptical look. "Well- maybe. But, I think that the River Walk would be nice. It would give us a chance to engage is conversation."

"The River Walk it is."

The River Walk was a 5-block long replica of the lower Mississippi river, from Cairo, IL, to New Orleans, LA. Along their journey, they actually revisited historical events and learned about geographical transformations.

"This is really nice," Dominique breathed in the cool, refreshing air.

"It is. I've been here a few times, but I've never enjoyed it as much as I'm enjoying it now," he told her.

"Really?"

"It must be the company. You know, you can really be quite charming, when you want to be."

"Ditto."

"I can honestly say that I understand the magnetism that draws men to you now. At first, I couldn't."

Dominique chuckled, a sound deep in her throat. "I don't know whether to take that as a compliment or an insult."

"Have you ever been in a deep relationship? I mean, a really serious one?"

"Nope. I don't usually allow men to get too close to me," she admitted.

"Why not?"

"I just don't. Maybe it's because-" She paused and took a deep breath. "Because of what happened to me when I was small."

"What happened?" he inquired, stumped.

"Remember at dinner when I told you that my mom had re-married but it didn't last long?" He nodded. "Well, the reason he left was because he was a pedophile. He began molesting me right away. I was ten years old."

"Damn." he exclaimed, truly shocked.

"He used such a clever ploy to lure children. I mean, who would think that a minister of the church would be a child molester?"

"That's some heavy shit."

"Well, if you think that's heavy, wait until I tell you the rest," she said cynically. "I never told my mama about the abuse. I just kept in inside. When it came out that he'd been touching on little boys and girls in the church, she asked me if he'd done anything to me. I lied and said he hadn't."

"Dominique, no." he groaned.

"I just couldn't tell her the truth. I felt so ashamed and dirty. I didn't want her to hate me or blame me."

"My God Dominique. I am so sorry that you felt you had to endure that all alone." He reached over and wiped away a tear that had escaped and slid down her cheek. "Come here."

She reluctantly went into his embrace. He rubbed her back and made soothing noises. Soon, she felt normal again.

"I'm okay," she said quietly, backing away. "Thank you."

"I guess you and me have a lot more in common than we thought," he told her. "We both have deep scars, unseen wounds. It may take a lifetime to heal them."

"I know," she said softly.

"Do you think you'll ever tell your mother?"

"I think I have to. It'll be the first step toward the healing process."

"I think it'll be a burden lifted from your shoulders. Dominique?"

"Yes?" She looked into his compassionate eyes.

"You know it wasn't your fault, right? What that sick bastard did to you and to those other innocent children, wasn't your fault."

"I keep thinking, if only I had told somebody then he wouldn't have been able to molest those other kids."

"You did what you felt was right. You were only a child." He put his arm around her shoulders. Now he felt like a true asshole for what he was thinking about doing to her. She'd been hurt by men all her life. Maybe

133

TERESA D. PATTERSON

that's why she used and discarded them. He didn't know if he had the heart to carry out what he'd previously planned. "Let's head back. You still feel up to bowling?"

"Yeah, of course. But, I've never bowled before," Dominique admitted.

"Never?"

"Nope."

"Well, there's nothing to it. I'll show you all the ropes." He gave her a reassuring squeeze and she smiled at him tentatively. Everything would be fine.

Dominique didn't know what she enjoyed the most, finally hitting one pin or the fact that Arvind had to press up against her, in order to show her how to hold the bowling ball. She really enjoyed herself. She felt much closer to him now that they'd both shared painful secrets.

"Thank you Arvind. I had a really good time," she told him as they headed for the car. The night's air was cool against their perspiration-dampened skins. Dominique inhaled and exhaled.

"I'm glad you had fun. But, remember, the night is still young. Now, I'm not sure if BB King himself is going to be at this club because he tours a lot. But, it should be nice, nonetheless."

"I'm actually looking forward to it," she said as he opened the passenger's door for her. She really meant that she was looking

forward to spending more time with Arvind.
She kept that thought inside though.

Dominique looked smashing in a black,
spaghetti-strapped evening gown. She'd
purchased it at Macy's and had never gotten a
chance to wear it. As she slid her stocking
covered feet into heels, she felt like Cinderella.

The tap at the door had her heart racing.
For some reason, excitement filled her. She
grabbed her small purse and shawl then went
to answer.

"You look really beautiful," Arvind
complimented upon seeing her. "You ready?"

"Yes," she said, closing the door behind
her. She looked him up and down in
appreciation. He had donned a cream colored
suit, complete with a tie. A stylish hat covered
his dreads. He could have just stepped off the
cover of *Damn Magazine*. She felt a twinge
between her legs.

Get your hormones together she warned
herself. She promised herself that she
wouldn't give in to her desires concerning
Arvind. If it was one thing she wanted from
him, it was respect. If she just hopped into the
bed with him that would just eliminate any
chance of that.

The club was packed but they were
directed to a table up front. When Dominique
sat down she raised a quizzical brow.

"I made reservations," Arvind explained.

"How thoughtful." She admired the scented candles burning in the middle of the table.

"I wanted your first time hearing and seeing someone performing the blues to be a memorable experience."

"That it is," she said as they sat back and enjoyed the first act. The club exploded with applause when the group had finished playing.

Dominique stopped applauding and picked up her drink.

"You look relaxed," Arvind remarked. "Is it because of the atmosphere or that drink you're sipping on?" he asked.

"A little bit of both," she giggled. "But, this drink is really good."

"Would you care for another one?"

"Well-" she hesitated stirring her straw around in the glass.

"You're not driving," he pointed out. "Besides, it's a fruity drink. There can't be that much alcohol in it."

"Okay, I'll take one more. But that will be it. I have a two drink limit," she explained.

"Good to know that you're not a lush." He signaled the waitress and ordered her another drink.

They got a special treat that night. BB King just so happened to be there and he put on an outstanding performance.

***

"That was amazing." Dominique exclaimed. Everyone filed out of the club wearing satisfied expressions on their faces. "I'll have to look for a similar type of environment back home."

"There are a few. I'll take you, if you'd like?" he offered.

"Name one place in Tampa where they play the blues live?"

"There are a few places. Of course we can always go to St. Pete. They have the Martini Bar. They have live blues and jazz. They also have a band that plays down at the pier. Then there's Gino's."

"Oh, I had no idea."

"Maybe you need to get out more. You mean to tell me that the guys you've dated haven't taken you out?" he asked in disbelief.

"No. It's usually all about sex for them," she admitted in a low voice.

Arvind stared at her deeply. "You're more than some man's piece of ass, Dominique," he told her straight forward. "You deserve to be treated better than that." Somehow, he really meant that. He continued to be torn about the decision he'd made to teach her a lesson.

Do I really? she asked herself but said nothing in response. She still couldn't understand why she felt wary of Arvind, but she did.

The next morning Dominique tried to figure out who was lying next to her in bed.

She felt a warm body pressed up against her back and saw a strong arm wrapped around her waist.

"What the fuck?" she exclaimed, when she looked over and saw that it was Arvind. "I didn't." she groaned aloud.

"Actually, you really didn't," he answered in sleep filled tones.

"Then why are you in my bed?"

"Correction, you're in *my* bed."

She sat up abruptly and immediately regretted it. Her head spun so fast that she thought it would fly off her neck.

"What the hell was in those two drinks?"

"I have no idea. But, you forgot your key and I didn't want to go back downstairs to get another copy because it was so late. Plus, I would have had to carry your drunken butt with me and I thought I'd spare you the embarrassment. If you'd unlocked the door between our two rooms, you could have slept in your own bed. But you didn't."

"Oh," she stated, holding her head. "Well, what time is it? Shouldn't we be getting up?"

"We?" He picked up a pillow and hit her with it softly.

"Arvind."

"You can get up. I'm going back to sleep."

"I need some coffee."

"There's a coffee pot and condiments right over there." He lifted a finger and pointed.

She got up. It was then that she realized what she had on. Another one of her black lace bra and panties sets. These had the boy shorts, which hugged her buttocks and allowed the cheeks to peek out a tad bit.

Arvind cracked open an eyelid and caught her walking towards the coffee maker. "Wow. Good morning." Immediately, he was full awake. At least a part below his waist had awakened.

"I thought you were going back to sleep."

"I can't now," he complained.

"Why not?"

"My dreams would be plagued with nothing but naughtiness."

Dominique turned her back and poured some coffee into a Styrofoam cup. "Do you want some cof-?" She caught herself. "Never mind." She remembered the time he'd tossed the coffee into the garbage.

"I'd better take a shower. Then I'll go down and get you another key," he said, sliding out from under the sheets. "Enjoy your liquid dirt."

"Enjoy your cold shower," she said knowingly. She'd seen the bulge in his boxers and knew without a doubt that he'd been aroused.

Chapter Eleven

Since they had time before his brother's wedding, they decided to visit the Memphis Zoo. Surprisingly, that idea came from Arvind.

"I don't care for smelly animals," Dominique said. "But, I have always wanted to see an elephant."

"You never went to the Laury Park Zoo in Tampa?"

"Never wanted to. I told you, I don't like stink." Her nose turned up as if smelling something bad.

"What about Sea World?"

"Isn't that where the whale is?" He nodded. "Stink. Probably smells like fish." She wrinkled her turned up nose.

"It's a whale. They don't smell fishy," he informed. "You don't even want to see the cute little dolphins?"

"Humph." is all she said.

"Well, I guess that would rule out you eating Sushi or Calamari, huh?"

"No. I'll try different types of food. That gets cooked."

"Some Sushi is served raw."

"I think I'd like it better smoked."

"Do you like seafood?" he asked.

"Love it."

"I'll keep that in mind," he said softly.

140

UNCROSSING HER LEGS

They had fun at the zoo. Arvind even got a disposable camera and took some pictures. Dominique struck a pose leaning against the elephant cage. The big gentle creature in the background seemed to be smiling.

***

The wedding went beautifully. Arvind looked extremely handsome wearing his tux as he stood next to his brother. The lovely bridesmaids wore lavender dresses that dipped down in the back. The beaming bride looked truly elegant. Her face glowed with happiness. Dominique found herself getting choked up and it wasn't even her relatives that were getting married.

After it ended, the photographer took lots of family photos. Dominique sat to the side and watched. Everyone seemed truly happy and it was obvious that the room was filled with so much love. The newly married couple kept hugging and kissing each other. She wondered if she'd ever have that type of bond with anyone.

Her eyes caught Arvind's. There was so much written there that she couldn't read. Could he be the type of man that could chase away her fears? Could he caresses her soul and calm her spirit? The most important question of all was could he ever love her?

Arvind was thinking along the same lines. He'd finally decided that he wouldn't go through with it. He wouldn't play games and hurt a woman that had already experienced so much pain. If Dominique wanted to sleep with men and never have anything meaningful in her life that was her business. Hell, if the men fell for the okey doke that would be on them.

Sunday morning they had prepared to attend church services with Arvind's aunt and uncle. They had gone downstairs to eat breakfast before leaving. Halfway through their meal, Arvind's cell phone rang.

"Hello?" When he dropped his fork in mid-air, Dominique knew that something was terribly wrong. "I'll be right there," he said in a voice filled with anguish.

"What is it?" His face had lost all of its coloring and his eyes looked haunted.

"It's my father. They found him in his home this morning."

"Is he okay? Arvind?" He didn't answer her straight away. "Arvind, is he okay?" she repeated, leaning over to touch him on his sleeve. "Arvind?"

"He's dead," he stated simply.

Arvind had insisted that she remain back at the hotel while he made the trip to Arkansas. However, Dominique wouldn't hear of it. He looked liked he would fall apart at any given moment. No way would she not be by his side. She'd even taken over driving the rental. All he had to do was give her the directions.

UNCROSSING HER LEGS

"He finally did it. He finally drank himself to death," Arvind said more to himself than to her. He stared out the window as they crossed the bridge between Tennessee and Arkansas. Gazing out over the waters of the Mississippi River, he found that he couldn't cry. He felt something. He just didn't know what.

"Would you like to talk about it?" Dominique asked softly.

"Nope," he declined. "I can't." He shook his head. The memories were just too painful. His parent's divorce had been the best thing that had ever happened to him. "Maybe- one day- maybe," he said.

Dominique reached over and clicked on the radio. The station was tuned to gospel so she decided to leave it there. They rode the rest of the trip in silence with the music playing softly in the background.

Arkansas was all that she'd thought it to be; country. She could see random chickens running around in different yards. She passed pastures of cows and horses as she drove on. They'd long since left Memphis, passing through West Memphis and Marion. Now they headed for a town called Lehi.

Some of the houses looked like tin roofed shacks. Dominique had no idea that people still lived in such poverty-stricken conditions. She saw someone getting water from a real pump. Just like on the show, *Little House on the Prairie.*

"What are those little houses in back of the big ones?" she asked, curiously. "Are they sheds?" She'd never seen such odd shaped storage units.

"Nope. They're bathrooms," Arvind answered.

"Oh." That blew her away and made her appreciate her own indoor plumbing all the more.

"Most people have modern facilities now. But, there are still a few who haven't upgraded. Make a left right here," he instructed so she did. "My kin folks live on Thompson's Road. They're way down at the end."

The drive wasn't as bad as he'd thought it would be. The narrow road had been paved, making it easier to travel. Arvind remembered a time when it hadn't been. As a kid, sometimes he had to trudge through slush and mud to make it to the highway for the school bus. In the winter, his grandfather had driven him on his tractor. One thing his dad had made sure of was that he got an education. He could thank him for that, if nothing else.

When Dominique brought the car to a stop he stared in awe. His grandparent's house had changed drastically. They'd torn down the old rickety, dilapidated structure that he'd known as a child. Now, there stood a modern, two-story redbrick home.

"I see they're living high on the hog," Arvind commented. "Not at all like the way I had to live." He remembered the freezing cold, non-insulated, two room shack that he'd grown up in.

He sighed. There was no reason to dwell on the past. His father had died and that was the real reason for his anger. Not that he thought that God's taking of the man was unfair. He didn't think that at all. He just wished it had happened a lot sooner. "I guess we'd better get out the car, huh?" he said.

"Yes."

"Well, I'm not going to wake up from a dream, so I guess I'd better just face it head on." He opened the door and got out. Dominique followed his example.

When they entered the living room a hush fell over the room.

"Vinny, I am so sorry for your loss," Aunt Bea said. Before he could move away, she'd enfolded him in her ample bosom. He remembered all those times when he'd run to her when he'd been a child. She'd always doctor up his scrapes and bruises or put a band aid on his wounds. Unfortunately, there was a band aid big enough for the open would in his heart now. He wanted to bawl like he did as a child, but he resisted the urge. Pulling away, he gazed at her. Aunt Bea was his father's sister. She had to be grief-stricken.

"Thank you. How are you holding up?" he asked her.

She gave him a sad smile. "The Lord saw fit to call him home. For that reason, I can't complain," she said simply, patting him on the back and going to take a seat on the couch.

He looked around. Everyone in the entire family seemed to have gathered together. Arvind hadn't thought that most of his relatives would have cared that his father had died. He'd isolated himself from just about everyone over the years. It went to show that blood really was thicker than water. Even though he had been a hard man to get along with, a difficult person, a wife-beater, a child-abuser, and a drunk, the kinfolks had still come to honor him in death.

Back at the hotel room, Dominique felt fatigued so she knew that Arvind had to be exhausted. He had talked with his family members for hours. She had seen the strain on his face throughout the entire evening.

She rapped gently on the door in-between the two rooms. It wasn't long before Arvind cracked it open and peered out.

"How are you holding up?" she asked.

"I'm fine. Come on in," he invited, opening the door wider. "It's not like I'm going to crack. Trust me, my father and I did not have that type of a relationship. I'm sorry this had to happen right now, though."

"Death is never predictable," she reminded him.

"It's just that, you and I were just getting to know each other. I'm going to have to remain for a while to make the funeral arrangements and take care of the burial. I'm afraid that you'll go back to putting up that wall and not let me in again. Hell, maybe you'll even decide to be with that Chad character."

"Arvind, that's not going to happen," she said. "You handle your family business. You and I can pick up when you get home."

"Can we pick up from here?" He crossed the room and tilted her chin. His lips claimed hers in a fierce kiss. It was filled with both longing and passion. Dominique struggled to breathe. He was surely drinking her soul, milking her spirit. She could feel her essence pouring into his heart. It seemed like they were fusing together and it was both wonderful and terrifying. "God, I want you." he groaned. Yet, he pushed her away.

"What is it?" she asked, flustered.

"Nothing. I just want our first time together to be special. Not because I'm grief-stricken – or whatever it is I am. I really want to be able to make love not just to you Dominique, but to your heart, your mind, your soul, and your spirit."

Dominique sat on the flight back to Tampa International alone. She couldn't stop

147

thinking about Arvind and praying that he'd be okay. Of course, he'd told her that he was holding up fine, but she didn't buy it.

Even if he and his father had the most awful relationship in the world, it was still family. The fact remained that the man who had helped to bring him into creation had died. That had to hurt. He had to be grieving.

Dominique had requested the keys to Arvind's car because she saw no reason for him to have to pay extra for parking. She'd pick him up from the airport upon his arrival. She'd get Lauretta to follow her and drop it off at his place and get a ride home. She'd already called Lauretta with the unhappy news about Arvind's father.

"Damn. He lost his uncle, now his father. That's so sad." She didn't mind being picked up by Dominique so that she could drop the car off. "Come on and pick me up so that you can fill me in on everything that happened."

Back in her apartment Dominique wandered around aimlessly. She'd tried reaching Arvind on his cell but kept getting his voice mail. She caught sight of herself pacing back in forth in her full-length mirror.

"What is the matter with you?" she asked herself. Could she be falling in love with Arvind Thompson? Never had she had such a strong reaction to another individual before.

The feelings were a bit premature to classify as love but she did know one thing, she cared for Arvind deeply. No one had ever touched her so profoundly yet he'd never laid a hand on her.

The phone rang and her heart leapt with joy. She picked it up on the first ring.

"Is everything okay? I've been trying to reach you all day," she said anxiously.

"What? My phone ain't rung." Her disappoint burned heavily in her gut when she realized it was Chad and not Arvind.

"Oh, Chad. What's going on?"

"I was jus' checkin' to see if you'd made it back. You still wanna have that talk? I mean I have a lot I need to get off my own chest. Can I come over?"

"Well, yeah. I guess it's okay."

"I'll be there in a few."

"Okay."

She hung up and sat on the couch to await his arrival. She didn't feel like entertaining him sexually so she'd didn't change into anything sexy. She kept on her polo jeans and shirt.

Chad looked handsome as usual in Roc-a-Wear gear. He didn't try to make any advances, just took a seat next to her on the couch.

"So, how was ya trip?" He began the conversation with small talk.

"Pretty good up until Mr. Thompson got the news that his father had died."

"Oh, damn. That's fucked up."

"Yeah, it is. But I know you didn't come here to talk about funerals. What's on your mind, Chad?"

He looked at her with a soft expression is his eyes. "You."

Dominique's heart began thumping furiously in her chest. This was always the most difficult part to ending her flings. However, in the past, none had gotten as attached to her as Chad obviously had. She realized at that moment that she really did like Chad and enjoyed his company.

"Chad, look-" she began.

"Naw, let me talk," he insisted. "I know I been trippin'. It's jus' that, I caught feelin's for you. I thought I could jus' deal wit' it bein' a sex thing. But, now that I think about it, I can't. The thought of somebody else fuckin' you – hell naw. I jus' go crazy thinkin' 'bout you wit' anybody else." His eyes bore into hers. "Dominique, I want you for me. I want you to be my main lady."

"Main lady?" Her mouth dropped open. It took a moment for his words to register. "What the fuck does *that* mean?" She'd had a speech all set for his ass until he'd dropped that bomb on her.

"Don't even trip. I mean you ain't the only one I'm fuckin'. Did you think that you was?"

Dominique had to sit completely up in order to soak in what he'd just told her. "You mean to tell me that, after all this pussy I've been giving you, you've been out in the streets fucking chicken heads, dirty-foots and nasty ass skanks?"

"Hey, hold up. Hold up. You ain't gotta put it like that. I'm selective in who I put my dick in."

"How many other women besides me are you fucking, Chad?"

"That ain't ya business. I jus' said I want you to be my main lady. So, that mean none of them others got nothin' on you. So why you trippin'?"

She stared into his face and realized that he was dead serious. "You son-of-a-bitch." She couldn't believe how much that realization hurt.

"Wait a minute. Now, you keep my mama outta this."

"Do you honestly, for one second, think that I'd be the type of woman to go for that shit?" She glared at him angrily. "Look me in my face, Chad. Do I look like a damn fool? Why the hell would I even accept something like that? Do I have *stupid bitch* tattooed on my forehead?"

"I thought you was feelin' me too. Don't you like what we have together?"

"We have nothing together." she snapped. "All we have is some great motherfucking sex. That's it."

"But I care about you."

"I *don't* care about you." she spat. "And I don't want anything more to do with you especially upon learning just *how much* you care. You care so much that you want to be with me *and* fuck other women." She stood up abruptly. "Chad, get out." She pointed towards the door.

"This ain't the way it was sup'ose to go down. I know I can't be wrong about how you feel. The way you be moanin' and screamin' when I got this good dick all up in you. I know you feelin' a brotha."

"Chad, what I was "feelin'," she mimicked. "Was your dick. Now get the fuck out."

"You gon jus' put me out like that?" He looked completely stunned.

"Yes," she said evenly. Their eyes locked.

"You know what, you a cold, heartless bitch." he insulted. "What you need is a man that's gone knock you side ya head all the time. I bet you'd like that."

"Are you threatening me?" Her eyes became mere slits.

"Naw, I ain't gotta stoop to that level. Besides, I wouldn't wanna risk hurtin' my baby."

"What the fuck are you talking about?" *This Negro has lost his damn mind.*

"You can diss me now, but you gonna want me when it's time to pay child support." With those words, he walked out and slammed the front door angrily.

Chapter Twelve

Chad obeyed Dominique's wishes and stopped dropping by. He did call once to ask how she was feeling. She thought that was strange but dismissed it. Even though she didn't particularly miss Chad she did miss the tongue-lashings he'd been giving her kitty cat. She remembered how he'd made her pussy purr. However, she caught herself before even attempting to pick back up where they'd left off. Chad had told her to her face that he fooled around with other women. She did not want to be caught up in his games. Besides, Tampa bitches were notorious for cutting each other up. The last thing she needed would be to get into some street brawl with a ghetto, ride-or-die type chick over some thug. She just had to write that dick off and go find another one.

Lately, she'd been going over her endless track record. More men had been inside her than Caucasian presidents in the White House. She had to slow down. She knew that part of her promiscuity came about from the molestation that had been forced upon her. She also knew that she didn't feel enough self-value to belong to any one man. She couldn't picture herself being with anyone long termed, let along becoming their wife. So, what would she and Arvind have once he got back into town? Would he accept just a sexual relationship or would he want more?

Arvind returned from his father's funeral looking as if all the life had been sucked out of him. Dominique tried to uplift his spirits by asking him out.

They went to a new movie starring Denzel Washington. Afterwards, Dominique invited him over to her place. She felt certain that Chad wouldn't show up since she hadn't heard from him in over a week. Even if he did, she would just have to handle it.

"Would you like a drink?" she offered as Arvind took a seat on the couch.

"Sure, I'll have some water."

"Alright." She retrieved a bottle of Zephyrhills out of the refrigerator and handed to him. She sat in the loveseat adjacent to him.

"Thanks." He screwed the top off and took a swig. "I appreciate your efforts of trying to get my mind off things." He leaned back into the couch cushions and exhaled. "It has definitely been a trying last few weeks."

"I can imagine."

"I guess in order for you to get to know the real me, I'll have to start at the beginning," he told her. "Are you ready for the biography of Arvind Leonard Thompson?"

"I'm ready."

"As you know, I was born and raised in Arkansas. For the first eight years of my life I witnessed by dad verbally, physically and mentally abuse my mom. I really think she was on the verge of a nervous breakdown at the point when my aunt stepped in and saved her. I remember that day like it happened yesterday." He frowned wryly. "My aunt and her boyfriend at the time had come to visit us. That itself should have sent up a red flag. But, my dad had been clueless. He'd gone off to work as usual. We had all piled into my aunt's boyfriend's car and left. Not before stopping by bank so that my mom could clean out his checking account. For so many years he had beat her down, destroyed her hopes and dreams, forced her to live in poverty, forbad her to continue her education, forced her to stop working whenever she got a job. He wouldn't buy her any new clothes only let her shop at Good Will or Thrift Shops. Many evenings we ate nothing but bologna because he only gave her $20.00 a week for groceries. She couldn't apply for any government assistance because he forbad that as well. Every evening when he'd come home from work, he'd start in on her. He'd call her just about every name in the book and he even made up some. He'd just about killed her spirit and mine too." He paused. "I was the laughing stock of my elementary school. I went to school every day looking like a throw-a-way kid. Dad wouldn't buy me any new clothes either." He stopped long enough to take another swallow of water. "Anyway, we

moved to Florida and began a new life. We
went to live with my great-grandmother, Mary
Corene Elizabeth Ruthie Mae Mitchell." He
smiled slightly. "Well, I guess since all Mama
knew was how to put up with abuse and
drunkenness, she got involved with one drunk
after another. She even ended up getting
married to another alcoholic, woman beater.
That marriage got annulled real fast. During
my junior year in high school, I went back to
live with my dad for the summer. I couldn't
get along with my mother's then-boyfriend. It
became obvious that Dad didn't want me
around. All he did was drink. That was the
year that I found out I had a brother. Mark
was the spitting image of my dad and me.
After I moved back here, Mark kept in touch.
He kind of gave me updates on Dad because I
never really tried to contact him and he didn't
call me."

"Not even on your birthday or holidays?"
Dominique asked quietly.

He shook his head. "Nope. I doubt if he
even remembered the day I was born."

"How sad."

"Well, it's all water under the bridge now.
He's dead. All I can say is, good riddance."

"Isn't there anything, anything at all that
you can find that was good about your
father?"

He seemed to think about it long and
hard. "No, I can't find one single thing."

"I know something that was good about him," she said. "He helped in the creation of you."

Arvind's eyes got moist. "Yeah, he created a son he didn't want." He cleared his throat and fell silent.

Dominique could feel his pain. She wanted to reach him and somehow erase the sadness. She got up and went to sit next to him. She placed her arm around his shoulder.

"Arvind just because your father didn't take in interest in your life, doesn't mean that you're not a remarkable human being. Despite all the abuse you endured growing up, you persevered. You're intelligent, kind-hearted and loving. You're respectful and you're a perfect gentleman, just to name a few."

His brow rose. "Perfect gentleman?"

"Yes, at least you have been up to this point."

"Would you rather for that to change?"

"That depends," she murmured huskily, catching the smoldering look in his eyes.

"Dominique, I play for keeps. I don't think you're ready for the likes of me," he warned.

"Maybe I'm not quite ready for you. But I definitely think I am ready for a change."

"Does this have anything to do with that guy you're seeing?"

"Was seeing, as in past tense. Actually, we ended it."

"He let you go, just like that?" he asked in disbelief. "He didn't flip out?"

157

"No, actually, I kind of lost it. He wanted me to be his "main" lady. I let it be known in no uncertain terms that I wouldn't stand for that. Then, I showed him the door."

"Good for you." He placed the bottle of water that he'd been holding on the table in front of him. Then he turned to face Dominique. "So, where do we go from here?"

"I'm not sure. Let's just take it one day at a time and see where that leads us."

The doorbell rang and Dominique groaned aloud. It better not be who she thought it was.

"Arvind, I'll be right back," she said, getting up.

"No problem."

Chad stood waiting on her welcome mat when she cracked the door open.

"Chad, I have company. I've asked you not to come by here without calling first."

"Get rid of that sucka," he demanded.

"The only person that's leaving is you." She tried to slam the door in his face but he blocked it from closing with his foot.

"What the fuck you think you doin'. I ain't goin' no where." He forced the door completely opened and stepped into her living room. Arvind, hearing the commotion stood up. "What the fuck he doin' here? I thought you said he was ya boss?"

"He is my boss. Chad, you are causing a scene. Please leave."

UNCROSSING HER LEGS

"I already tol' you. I ain't goin' no fuckin' where. But this bitch better bounce up outta here befo' I really show my ass."

"As if you aren't already?" Dominique didn't know what to do. She had assumed that Chad had gotten the point that they were through. Obviously, he hadn't. She turned to face Arvind. "I'm sorry about this."

"I thought that the two of you had ended things. This doesn't look like the end to me," he said accusingly. Another quality of a bitch, she'd juggle two men if she had to. Damn, he had been thinking about other men falling for the okey doke and he'd fallen for it himself.

"I- I don't know what to tell you." She sighed audibly.

Chad took a seat and began behaving as though he lived there. He picked up the remote and then stretched out on the couch. Dominique rolled her eyes.

"I guess I'd better leave you two at it. But, not before I tell you this one thing. You can't make room for the new, Dominique, until you get rid of the old baggage."

"Punk, who the fuck you callin' luggage?" Chad got up from his reclining position.

"I said baggage. There's a difference," Arvind spoke in a clipped tone.

"Oh, what's up then bitch? You wanna step to me wit' that fuck shit?"

Arvind shook his head. "Man, I swear, you are so uncouth."

TERESA D. PATTERSON

"You usin' big words and shit, like I don't know what you talkin' 'bout. Punk, you tryin' to insult my intelligence or what?"

"Both of you just stop it." Dominique intervened. "Y'all need to remember exactly where you are. Respect my fucking place." She wanted to say more but suddenly a feeling of nausea washed over her. "Ugg. I don't feel so good."

"What's wrong?" Both men asked in union.

"I don't know-" She felt the bile rush up in her throat and ran out of the room.

While Dominique was out the two men eyed each other.

Fake ass, frontin' ass bitch. Chad thought.

Punk ass thug-wanna-be, baggy pants wearing motherfucker Arvind thought.

Bourgeois ass, suburban bitchified, metrosexual pussy-ass ho Chad smirked.

Weak gangsta, po' pimpin', baby mama havin', gettin' chased by the po-po, crack cocaine slingin bitch Arvind smirked back.

"Shouldn't you be headin' home to Brokeback Mountain?" Chad tossed his way.

"That's real classy. Where did you get it, Mother Goose?" Arvind threw up his hands. He didn't have time for this shit. He could see if he was fighting for a woman worth having. Apparently, Dominique wasn't that type of woman. "Hey, look I'm going to be the bigger man and just leave. At least I have sense

160

enough to understand that this is an awkward situation for her. Tell her I say good night."

Chad waited until he got to the door. "Yo, um, what's ya name? Do us both a favor and don't come back."

When Dominique returned and found Arvind gone, her heart sank. She really wasn't in the mood to go through it with Chad. Telling him to leave would just make him want to stay.

"Chad, I'm really tired and I think I ate something that doesn't agree with me. Can we do this tomorrow?"

"That's cool wit' me," he surprised her by saying. "As long as that busta's gone, I ain't got no issues."

"Chad, you cannot govern my life. I thought I made it clear to you that I did not want to be one of your bitches."

"I don't want you to be one of my bitches. Jus' be my ho for life."

"If you meant that to be a joke, it's not funny."

"I was jus' playin'. Damn, you mighty sensitive." He stared at her with a strange light in his eyes. "I know what's wrong wit' you."

"Exactly what do you know?" She was feeling so tired all of a sudden and his keeping her from bed made her irritated.

"You knocked up."

"What?"

"Pregnant. You're carryin' my baby."

"Chad, don't even play like that. We have always used protection."

"Have we?" So, poking holes in the condoms hadn't been necessary. He had already done what he'd planned- planted his seed.

"Yes we have." she snapped. "God Chad, I am trying not to be a bitch but that's kind of difficult with you. Damn it I'm tired. Go home."

"Okay. I'm out. But call me when you get the test results back. "

Tuesday rolled around and Dominique picked up the phone to call her mother. She knew she'd be expecting her to pick her up for their usual walk. For some reason, she felt that it was time to talk to her about the past.

"Mama, I'm calling to cancel our walk. But, there's something I need to tell you."

"What is it Nikki?"

"I can't discuss it on the phone. Is it okay for me to come over?"

"Of course. You know you're welcomed here any time."

"I'll be there in a few. Bye."

"Bye."

Telling her mom that her husband had sexually molested her would be so hard to do. Yet, she felt compelled to let the secret out. She knew she'd be stuck in a continuous cycle until she let go of all the pain. In order to do that, the truth had to be told.

Mrs. Green had set out some muffins and poured Dominique a steaming cup of coffee when she sat down at the kitchen table.

"So, what's going on?" she asked.

Dominique didn't know where to start. She looked around the kitchen that had held such fond memories before Jessie had destroyed them. He began pinching her buttocks while she stood at the sink washing dishes. She'd been ten-years-old.

"Mama, I- I lied to you," she managed to say. Before she could continue the tears slipped unchecked down her cheeks.

"What is it baby? What about? Please tell me." Her mother got up and grabbed her in such a fierce hug. "What is it?"

"I lied about Jesse not touching me. He did." she blurted out through her tears. "He touched me every chance he got. And when I turned twelve- he r-r-raped me."

"Oh Lord Jesus. Why didn't you tell me child? Why?" Her mother wailed.

"I didn't want you to hate me. I thought you'd say it was my fault. That's what Jesse told me."

"Oh Lord. Lord. Aw, have mercy. Forgive me baby. Please forgive me for not being the type of mother that you could come to," she sobbed. "My baby. My poor baby."

"It wasn't your fault. I love you, Mama. It wasn't your fault." The two held and rocked

163

each other for quite some time, crying and just letting it all out.

When they had both calmed down a bit, Dominique got up and poured her cup of cold coffee into the sink. She fixed another one.

"I wanted to come back home but I just couldn't set foot in the place where I'd been abused for so many years." She put her coffee down and hugged her shoulders. "He'd take me in the bathroom and I'd have to look at the picture of Jesus while he did his business. I felt so ashamed. It was just like in that movie *The Color Purple*. He said, '*You better not tell nobody but God.*'"

"I guess God kept me in the dark for a good reason because He knows my heart. He doesn't place any more on us than we can bear. If I had found out about something like that, I would have ended up on death row." She poured herself a fresh cup of coffee as well. "Jessie would have been good and dead so he couldn't have ruined anybody else's child."

"I figured as much, so I kept it a secret."

"Well, Jessie got what he deserved. You know how they feel about child molesters in prison. They ganged up on him, raped him, beat him up pretty bad, too."

"I never heard about that."

"He contracted AIDs because of the gang rape, and died a slow, miserable death behind bars." She shook her head. "God don't like ugly."

UNCROSSING HER LEGS

"I guess I should feel sorry for him, but I don't," Dominique said quietly.

Chapter Thirteen

Dominique felt like she'd been hit in the stomach and had all the wind knocked out of her. She gasped audibly. The Asian doctor with the shiny hair cut in a bob stared at her strangely.

"Are you okay?" she asked in her accent, concern written on her face.

"W-what did you just say?" Dominique stammered.

"I said, the reason you're so sick is probably because you're expecting," Dr. Lynn Wong repeated, glancing down at Dominique's chart. "Yes. Based on your last monthly cycle and the urine test, you're about six weeks pregnant."

"Oh my God." Now it all added up. All the strange comments Chad had been tossing her way. That no good bastard had done it on purpose. But, she couldn't understand how. She knew that he'd put a condom on every time that they'd gotten busy. She wracked her mind trying to figure out how it could have happened.

"Baby not so good news?" Dr. Wong questioned. "I have pamphlets." She handed Dominique several pamphlet on childbirth, adoption and abortion. Dominique took the pamphlets, tucked them into her purse. She thanked the doctor then left.

UNCROSSING HER LEGS

She walked out of the OB/GYN office in a daze. What the fuck would she do with a baby? She had never really thought about being a mother. For as long as she could remember, she'd never been too fond of children. Everybody that she knew who had kids never had time for anything. When they did have time, they never had money. Children left you broke.

And the fact that Chad would be the father didn't sit too well with her. She didn't want a drug dealer to be her baby's daddy. Hell, she didn't want a baby daddy. How in the hell could it have happened?

She knew she should have stayed on the birth control pills. Even though the pill had given her migraines, she could have dealt with that instead of this news. The Depo Provera shot had made her bleed for six months, but she'd gladly bleed for an eternity if it meant not getting knocked up by the wrong man.

What in the hell would she tell her mother? It hadn't been too long ago that her mother had been asking about grandchildren. But her mother had expected a husband to be in the picture.

Suddenly, Arvind came to mind. They could have no future with another man's baby in the way. She'd have to get rid of it. She just couldn't risk a baby running everything she'd worked so hard for. Not to mention the fact that it would wreck havoc on her figure. No way would she welcome pushing something heavier than a bowling bowl out of her cunt.

As she drove towards home, she weighed the pros and cons. She definitely did not have room for a child. She'd have to move into a bigger place. She'd have to trade in her car for one that had more than two seats. Could she give up her Mercedes for a baby?

Would it be fair to Chad if she aborted his baby without telling him? Even she couldn't be that heartless. Could she put herself through something as emotional as an abortion? She'd heard about it and had never thought she'd have to make such a choice. If she decided to have the baby, what if Chad wanted custody of the child? He wouldn't just sign away his rights if she wanted to give the child up.

"I guess the person to talk to is Chad." She pulled up to her apartment and went inside. Picking up the phone, she dialed Chad's number.

Dominique wanted to smack the black off Chad. She had remembered what Lauretta had told her about some men sabotaging the condoms Something had prompted her to check the box of Magnums in her nightstand drawer. She'd found out that each pack had small pinholes stuck through it.

She paced back and forth while she waited for him to arrive. She wanted to scream at the top of her lungs or throw something. Damn, she wanted to turn over furniture.

When Chad got there she fought to hold back her fury. She would not lose it and end up in the Hillsborough County Jail. She had to handle it in a civilized fashion. After all, she was still a lady, pregnant or not.

"What up?" he greeted, sitting down.

"Chad, I went to see my gynecologist today and guess what she told me?" She stood glaring at him, with her hand on her hips.

"Nothin' I ain't already know," he stated matter-of-factly.

"I'm sure you *did* know since you've been poking holes in the motherfucking condoms," she yelled.

He chuckled. "I guess you found out, huh? Oh well, so now what?"

"What the fuck do you think? I'm going to the next available appointment to take care of this situation."

Chad sat up. "Situation? What the fuck you talkin' 'bout, "take care of the situation?" I know you ain't sayin' what I think you sayin'?"

"If you're thinking abortion, that's exactly what I'm saying."

"Hold up. Hell to the fuck naw. You ain't killin' my seed. You mus' been done lost ya damn mind up in here."

"You're the one who's lost it. Chad, I didn't ask for you to get me pregnant. You tricked me. And that's not right. Having sex with you was all good. Even dealing with your shows of jealousy was something I could handle. But, I never once told you or anybody else for that matter, that I wanted children. This crosses the line."

"Well, it's too fuckin' late now, ain't it? Grow the fuck up Dominique. And start thinkin' about somebody else besides ya self," he tossed at her. "That's a motherfucking innocent baby. I ain't gonna jus' let you kill my kid."

"How can you stop me?"

"I got ways. But, I'm not gonna even hafta go there. That's my baby and I know that wit'out a doubt. I want my son."

"How the fuck you know it's going to be a boy?"

"Because I put it down like that."

"Whatever Chad." she snapped. She was so angry she wanted to slap him across his face.

"Look at it this way, the shawty ain't neva gonna want for nothin'. I make mad money," he said.

"I don't care about how much income you're making. It's your lifestyle that concerns me. What type of an example can you set for a child?"

Chad grew silent. "Hell, I could go back to school and finish my degree. I only got six credits left before I get my bachelor's. Then I can get a real job. I told you from the jump that I wasn't gonna be in the drug game for

long. I jus' needed a reason to leave it alone."
He gave her a serious look. "Now, I got a
reason—two reasons."

Dominique felt torn. On one hand, she
could understand where Chad was coming
from. Really, there was no reason for her to
have an abortion. Simply not wanting a child
was selfish, if she considered it fully. Besides,
she couldn't even say that she didn't *want* a
child. She just hadn't ever thought about
having one, the reason behind that being her
selfishness

Could she do as Chad advised and
consider someone other than herself for a
change? She seriously doubted she could go
through with an abortion anyway. Just
thinking about her mother and how it would
hurt her made Dominique wary of making
such a final decision right away.

If having a baby could make Chad turn his
whole life around, would she want to be with
him? She tried to picture them living together
as a family but couldn't. The fact remained
that she didn't love Chad.

She stood before the large mirror over her
dresser and stared at herself. "I'm pregnant,"
she said. She didn't look or feel any different.
She gazed to the left at the full-length mirror
and placed her hands on her stomach. "How
will I look in three months? Five? Wow." The
idea of her carrying and bearing a child
almost overwhelmed her and she sat on the

edge of her bed. "I'm having a baby," she said aloud. Speaking the words made it all too real.

Well, it would be a while before she began showing. Until then, she would tell no one. Regardless of what Chad wanted, it was her body and she had a right to choose.

Chapter Fourteen

Arvind kept trying to figure out what was bothering Dominique. Since his encounter with Chad at her apartment, she seemed to be avoiding him. At work she remained cordial, but he didn't sense the same warmth she'd shown when they'd been away on their trip. It had to be Chad. He wouldn't let a low-life like that get in the way of what he had to do.

He should have kicked Chad's ass but he hadn't wanted to start any drama in Dominique's home. He really couldn't understand the attraction. Why did some women go for the losers when they had a decent man with goals and good benefits?

He had pegged Dominique correctly- gold-digger. Sleeping with a drug dealer was something a low-morale chicken head would do. Chad must be working with a monster to keep a sex-fiend like Dominique coming back.

Well, regardless of how Chad got-down in the bedroom, Arvind knew that he could run a ring around him. He'd have Dominique climbing the walls.

He'd been nice long enough. For months now, he'd been nothing but a gentleman. He'd been holding off on bedding down Dominique. It was time to step his game up. She would be one conquest that he would enjoy immensely.

If one dozen roses could melt her—he'd find out what two-dozen of long-stemmed red roses would do. The greedy bitch would probably cream in her panties. He knew she thought that he rolled in money. The fact was, Troutman Investments and Mutual Funds were about to go under. And when the company folded, Dominique would crumble right along with it. He wasn't Captain Save a Ho, so it didn't matter to him. He would, however, be glad to tap that ass before it happened, though.

Dominique sat at her desk lost in thought. Seeing the delivery man carry a bunch of roses sent a shiver of anticipation through her.

"Miss Dominique Green?"

"Yes?"

"These are for you." He placed the beautiful flowers on her desk.

"Thank you."

"Have a nice day ma'am."

"You, too."

She reached for the card and smiled when she saw Arvind's signature.

Lately, she'd been so torn. She'd been trying to figure things out on her own. She still had no idea what she was going to do about the baby. All she knew is that she wanted to be with Arvind. They'd just take it one day at a time.

When she got the call from LeMarquis Vanderdol, she saw it as a way to win Arvind over. If she secured such a major account for

UNCROSSING HER LEGS

Troutman Mutual Funds and Investments, Arvind would be so proud of her. Never did she think that it would all blow up in her face.

Arvind had made the right decision about Dominique. She'd blown any chances of ever gaining his respect. Someone had witnessed her coming out of the Sheridan Hotel with LeMarquis Vanderdol and relayed the information to him. Arvind was so furious that he wanted to wring her neck. LeMarquis Vanderdol was their main competitor and had tried a hostile take-over of Lauderdale two years prior. Dominique had a lot of explaining to do and he couldn't wait until she returned. Did the woman have no shame? He thought that in the last few months they had grown closer. She'd indicated that she wanted more than the frequent bootie calls and the meaningless flings. He remembered a phrase his friend Javon used to say, "You can't turn a ho into a housewife." Why even bother to try?

The door to Arvind's office was cracked. Dominique didn't know whether to walk in or wait to be invited. She could see Arvind pacing back and forth and that wasn't a good sign. She tapped lightly and pushed the door open.

"Brenda said you wanted to see me?"

"I don't know what type of game you're playing but it better not cause Lauderdale to pull out." he exploded. "You know LeMarqis

Vanderdol is our rival company as well as Lauderdale's." Dominique eyes widened as he continued to rant. "Miss Green, you really should be a bit more discreet. If you're going to carry on in such a fashion, do it where no one from Troutman Investments can see you."

"I have no idea what you're talking about and I'm not playing games," she finally said.

"You're putting our professional reputation on the line by hooking up with our competitor. If word of this gets back to Jack, do you think he'll want to remain signed with us? You're sleeping with the enemy, for Christ's sake. Could you have at least waited for the ink to dry on the papers that Jack Lauderdale signed, first?"

Dominique was starting to get irritated. Arvind had thrown all kinds of accusations at her and she didn't know why. All she'd done was what Troutman Investments was paying her to do, secure accounts.

She slapped a signed contract from Vanderdol Investments on his desk. "Instead of riding my ass with this criticism, can you open your mouth with a word of praise?" she snapped. "I just got us another major account."

Arvind took a seat and tried to maintain some form of control. He picked up the contract and flipped through the pages. Then he looked at Dominique with disgust.

"You may have gotten another huge account, but is it worth your self respect?

Does it excite you to sleep with the highest bidder?"

Before she knew it, her palm had connected with his cheek.

"How dare you sit there and call me a whore to my face. I've never slept with any of our clients to close a deal. I didn't do it in the past and I don't have to do it now." She got in his face. They were so close that he could see the ring around her iris. "Yes, I have a pussy, Mr. Thompson, and I know how to use it. But I don't mix business with pleasure. Regardless of what you may think, I earned this account. Before you open your mouth to insult me again, get your fucking facts straight. I may be a slut, but I'm not anybody's whore."

"Dominique, wait," he said, but she stalked out of his office, this time, letting the door slam behind her.

Chapter Fifteen

Since the evening that Dominique had told Arvind off, he had stayed a safe distance away. He didn't require her to work late nights because they'd secured the Lauderdale account and had nothing to worry about.

Now she stayed late because the truth was, she would be bored at home alone. Since she'd given Chad the boot, her nights were lonely and unfulfilled. She spent so many hours with her vibrator that she'd named it. Bradley needed a new set of batteries. It was a miracle that she hadn't short-circuited the thing from all the extra usage.

Thinking about masturbating made her sigh from frustration. She needed a man. She wanted someone to pound her love box until she experienced back-to-back orgasm. Then he could turn her around and take her from the back. If he slapped her on both ass cheeks as he plunged in and out of her that would be an added bonus.

"Ugg." She groaned and got up from her desk. She walked over to the window and stared out into the rainy night. As she looked at the sky a streak of lightening caused her to jump in alarm. "Let me go before it really starts up."

Back at her desk she gathered up her belongings. She slid the documents she'd been working on into her briefcase. She'd go

178

over them during the weekend. After all, she had plenty of time on her hands.

Dominique stepped into the elevator. Just as the doors were about to close, someone's arm shot through causing them to reopen.

Arvind. Her heart dropped. He was the last person she wanted to see.

Dominique automatically stepped back. She and Arvind had few words to say to each other as of late. She'd never admit it, but he'd hurt her feelings with his insinuations and accusations.

"Wet night," he commented.

"Yep," she said, as the elevator moved.

"Think we'll make it to our cars before the downpour?"

"You shouldn't worry Mr. Thompson. You have the luxury of parking under the covered garage," she remarked somewhat sarcastically.

"Maybe soon you'll be parking there too," he said.

Dominique made no comment. Only presidents, vice-presidents, and CEOs got to park in reserved spaces. She was neither and at the rate she was going, she'd be lucky if she didn't get fired.

The lights flickered. They went off and came back on.

"Oh." Dominique exclaimed. The lights flickered again. This time when they went out they didn't come back on. The elevator lurched and came to an abrupt stop.

"We can't be stuck." Arvind groaned. He felt himself break into a cold sweat.

Dominique stepped forward and pressed some of the buttons. Nothing.

"I think that's exactly what we are. Stuck like Chuck. I'll try to call for help." She tried her cell phone but kept getting a busy tone. "I can't dial out."

"I'll try mine." Arvind did the same thing to no avail. "Nope." In the enclosed compartment, neither could get any reception. "Damn." Arvind swore. He hated small, cramped spaces. He couldn't breathe. Well, he could breathe but his mind had convinced him that he couldn't. He had to get out before Dominique witnessed him breaking down. He couldn't allow that to happen. She already saw him as an overbearing, opinionated asshole. The last thing he wanted was for her to see him in a vulnerable state. He had to think of something. He gazed up at the trap door in the ceiling.

"I can lift you up and you can crawl out," he told her. "Then you can go to the office and use the phone to call someone."

"Good idea," she said. At this point, she'd try anything. She just needed to get as far away from Arvind as she could. Her hormones raged out of control and she didn't want to make a fool out of herself by jumping his bones. "Come on, let's do this." She took off her heels and he boosted her up into the air.

"Push with all your might," he instructed so she did. The door gave way and she pushed it to the side. She hoisted herself up into the opening. "Hurry." she heard him say as she crawled along. She was above the ceiling of someone's office. She didn't care whose it was as long as it had a phone. She slid back the vent and climbed out. It wasn't a long drop but she felt it in her ankles and shins. She'd have to use a chair to climb back up because she didn't have Arvind to give her a boost.

Testing the phone she found a dial tone. "Good." She dialed 911 and immediately heard. "Hello, what's is your emergency?"

"We're stuck in the elevator. Well, at least my boss is. He helped me out so that I could use the phone to call for help," she explained.

"I'll alert the fire department. What is your location, ma'am?"

Dominique went through all of the preliminaries then drugged a chair from the desk to climb back into the vent. She crawled to the opening in the elevator and stared down. She saw Arvind in the far corner curled into a fetal position. He whimpered softly. Her heart twisted.

"Arvind," she called gently. "It's okay. Help is on the way." He didn't respond. She found herself crawling back down the entryway. "I'm here. It's okay." She touched his back to find him trembling. She remembered how he'd reacted on the plane and knew he was having an attack of claustrophobia. She could be

181

sympathetic and croon to him like he was a baby, but she felt that he was too far-gone for that. So, she tried a less subtle approach.

"Arvind you've got to pull it together. In a few minutes a bunch of firemen will be here to rescue us. You don't want them to find you like this, do you?" He didn't answer, just continued to whimper. "I mean, they will probably be manly, strong, attractive- and sexy as hell in their uniforms They'll find you all tucked into yourself, sweating like a runaway slave. What kind of image is that?" She paused, but he still didn't answer. He'd stopped whimpering, though. "You're the CEO. You don't want to be wearing a greasy, puke face if they post your picture on the front of tomorrow's paper. Get up."

"You sure know how to boost a brother's ego," he finally said, lifting his head.

"You know how I am. Just keeping it real."

"Yeah, I know." He managed to sit up. He pressed his back against the wall of the elevator. His breath came is gasps. Gradually, his breathing returned to normal. "Am I really sweating that badly?" he asked, thinking about the comment she'd made. When he allowed himself to let everything sink in, he began to chuckle. It had to be funny looking at it from someone else's perspective. Him, the CEO of a major company, balled up in the corner of an elevator, almost in tears because of a damn phobia. He shared his thoughts with Dominique and they both laughed.

"Dominique, you know, I really owe you an apology- again. I spoke with LeMarquis Vanderdol and he let me know in no uncertain terms that I was dead wrong in my assumptions. The man has nothing but respect and admiration for you," he went on to say. "I judged you and I was wrong for that. Can you ever forgive me?"

"It's nothing," she lied. "I'm used to it anyway."

He could tell by the way she avoided his eyes that it did matter. It occurred to him that Dominique Green was hiding more than just a sexy body beneath her outrageously expensive suits and high priced facials. She was hiding the fear of not being accepted, of not being good enough.

"Dominique, you know true beauty starts on the inside and works it way out," he said softly.

Dominique knew what he thought of her. She was beautiful on the outside, but ugly on the inside. Selfish, spoiled, used to getting her way. She was shallow and superficial. She didn't really care about other people's feelings. Well, she hadn't until recently. She cared about what Arvind thought. For some reason, his opinion mattered a great deal. But, it would never happen. Arvind would never look at her the way he looked at a woman he desired. She probably repulsed him.

It startled her when she felt his hand close around hers.

"Come here."

"Arvind–"

"Shh. Come over here and make me forgot about being trapped in this small ass box. I'm better but I'm not one hundred percent. I certainly wouldn't want those firemen who resemble male-strippers to find me punking out."

Dominique slid next to him. Automatically, his arm went around her shoulder. She searched her mind for something witty to say but couldn't find anything appropriate so she just kept quiet.

"You know, I'm so glad you don't wear those short skirts anymore," he said, breaking the silence. "Just imagine what you would have looked like climbing over my shoulders in something like that. I would have seen everything. Especially when I pushed you up through that opening." He had to make himself stop because of the vision that came into his head.

"Arvind."

"I'm serious. I would have forgotten all about my claustrophobia in a second. You probably wear those little, Victoria Secret type thingys, huh?"

Dominique couldn't hide her smile. She actually did frequent Victoria Secrets. She purchased all of her fine lingerie there as well as scented lotions.

"What are you wearing now? Humor me. Take my mind off of this." He waved his hands in the air for emphasis.

"You humor me. What do you wear, boxers or briefs?" she asked, teasingly.

"Boxers. I can't have my boys all squeezed together. They have to have room to breathe." Dominique threw her head back and laughed. This was a side of Arvind that she'd never seen. It was a side that she wanted to see more of.

"Arvind, I didn't know you had such a sense of humor," she said.

"There are a lot of things you don't know about me, Dominique. Like, what I think about every night while I'm lying alone in my king-sized bed."

"What do you think about?" she whispered, her heart thumping in her chest.

"About you. About that first day when you were sitting in my uncle's office crossing and uncrossing your legs. What I wanted to do to you then. What I want to do to you now."

"Yeah? And exactly what is that?"

"I think I can show you better than I can tell you." He pulled her onto his lap. "I wish you did have on a short skirt now."

"It's not my fault. You're the one who decided to change the dress code," she reminded him.

"That's because I knew it would torture me every day to see you walking around in those sexy ass skirts."

"So, tell me, what did you want to do to me?" she asked boldly.

He stared deeply into her eyes before answering. "I wanted to taste you." His words sent shivers down her spine. She swallowed, suddenly nervous. Never had she been so intimidated by a man, but Arvind wasn't just any man. He was the one man that she hadn't been able to impress. He hadn't fallen under her spell. Now, he was revealing that he'd been just as interested in her as she'd been in him. She had him right where she wanted him. She could do one of two things: fuck the shit out of him and kick him to the curb, which was customary. Or she could give him something to look forward to. Entice him. Maybe he'd stick around. She decided on the latter.

She found herself unzipping his fly. She could feel his member straining against the boxers he wore. When she touched him there, she was impressed. Arvind wasn't a small man by far. This was going to be a pleasure for both parties involved.

Dominique knew exactly what she was doing. She didn't have a set of luscious, full lips to let them go to waste. She'd learned earlier in her sexual conquests that sometimes you had to do some extra special things to impress rich men. They were used to gold diggers who'd do anything for some change.

UNCROSSING HER LEGS

But not Dominique. She dished out her favors and got everything she wanted in return. She'd been given condos, expensive cars, jewelry and furs- all because she had what men wanted and they were more than willing to pay her for it.

When she'd satisfied those men, it had all been a game to her. She'd wanted to give them a mind-blowing experience in order to get something out of it. But now, she just wanted to please. She wanted to give Arvind the most pleasure he could ever possibly receive.

Dominique had made it a point to never swallow. But for some reason, she didn't want to waste a drop of Arvind's sweet nectar. She couldn't believe how much kept spewing forth. She kept gulping it down only to feel more shoot to the back of her throat.

The thought of swallowing his seed turned her on so much that she reached an orgasm. She could feel the muscles between her legs clench and unclench and she gasped as she took every inch of him in her mouth. She milked him until she felt the throbbing cease and he gradually deflated.

When it was over Arvind leaned back, panting. "That was something else." he breathed.

Dominique was speechless. She hadn't gotten past the fact that she had actually swallowed a man's jism. Even more, she had enjoyed it.

Before the firemen came to their rescue, the lights in the elevator snapped back on. They heard loud noise and once again everything was in working order.

"I guess you won't get to see any sexy firemen after all," he teased pushing the button for the first floor.

"I've had enough excitement for one night anyway."

"Really? That's too bad, I thought you'd give me a chance to return the favor," he said suggestively.

"Well, when you put it like that, your place or mine?"

"Which is closer?"

"Your office."

"Arvind, how are you going to get any work done?" she asked once they had finished. "Every time you sit at this desk, you're going to be distracted," she said.

"Oh, that's something that the new CEO will have to contend with," he told her, pulling on his pants. *If there is a new CEO.*

"New CEO?" Her fingers stopped on a button and she glanced up.

"Yes. Remember, I was only filling in for my uncle. I never intended to make running Troutman Investments my main priority."

"Oh. So, does that mean you're leaving?"

UNCROSSING HER LEGS

"I'll be going back to run my own business." He looked her up and down. "Enough talk about business. Would you like to go to my place or yours?"

"Mine."

Chapter Sixteen

Arvind made love to Dominique several times until they were both completely worn out. Dominique had finally found a man who could out freak the freak in her. She had definitely met her match in the bedroom.

"Dominique, you know I really enjoy this chemistry thing that we have going here," he told her. He was serious. The bitch had a mouthpiece and could suck the hell out a dick. Her pussy was banging too. Hell, he might just keep her around.

"I feel the same way Arvind. But before you say anything else, I have to tell you something."

"Sounds deep," he said, leaning on his elbow and watching her intently.

"I don't know how to say this, well- I'm pregnant with Chad's baby. I've been contemplating abortion but it's really not what I want." Arvind sat in silence. Dominique exhaled slowly. "It began out as a sex thing. During the course of it, I did start to care about him. When I found out that he'd been poking holes in the condoms, it made me furious. I wanted nothing more to do with him. Then, I discovered that there was a child growing inside of me, his child. I can't hate him. I think he has a right to be a part of his child's life."

She looked at his face and it was formidable. "What are you saying? Are you thinking about keeping the child? I don't know why you're even hesitating on getting rid of that bastard. You should have been to the nearest abortion clinic like yesterday. Do you really want to pro-create with that fucking deadbeat?"

"Arvind, you don't even know Chad." Surprising herself, she came to Chad's defense.

"And you do? The man poked holes in the damn condoms, for heaven's sake. He sells drugs for a living. He's not exactly Father of the Year. Why would you even consider having a child with *that*?"

"That? He's a human being, not a that." For some reason, she was beginning to get angry. How could a man that she thought she knew change so fast right in front of her eyes?

"Dominique, you and I, we can have something. But not if you're saddled down with another man's brat. I can honestly tell you that I will not accept another man's child as my own."

Dominique stared at him in shock. "I can't believe you're saying this to me."

He reached for her and she dodged his touch. "Baby- I'm just saying."

"Don't fucking touch me." She got out of the bed and glared down at him. "You are not God. You have no right to judge anyone. And what gives you the right to suggest that I abort another man's baby?"

Arvind smirked. "I could see if he really was a man. But that Chad character is a loser, Dominique."

She stared at him long and hard. Had the sensitive man that she'd grown to care about disappeared? Had he been fronting the entire time? "The real loser turns out to be you, Arvind. I would like for you to get dressed and leave," she said quietly.

"What?"

"I want you to go. Us hooking up, it was the biggest mistake I ever made in my life." She looked into the face that she'd once thought was so charming and appealing. "Good-bye, Arvind."

"If I walk out that door Dominique, that's it. It'll be over for good. There will be no turning back. Is that what you really want?"

"Yes."

He made no move to get up. "You mean to tell me that you'd choose a man with no real job over me?"

"I'm not choosing anyone. I'm thinking of the future of my child."

"If you get the fucking abortion, there will be no child in the future." he exploded causing Dominique to jump. "It's for the best."

"You don't know what's best for me. But, I know what's best for you," she said evenly. "Get the fuck out my damn bed Negro. If you don't leave now, I will turn into the bitch that you hate."

Arvind jumped up and began pulling his clothes on angrily. "You know something, to be so damn educated, you're one simple minded bitch."

"What the fuck did you just call me?"

"You heard right. You black bitches are all the same. You say you want a good man, then you trip when you get one. Well, you know what Miss High and Mighty Bitch, see if you and lover-boy Chad can raise the little bastard on no income. I'm downsizing the company and your position will no longer be needed."

"You're firing me?" she asked in total disbelief. "You can't do that. I'll slap a lawsuit on your ass so quick that your fucking head will spend."

"Go right ahead. Downsizing isn't illegal."

"Troutman Investments is growing. Why would you need to downsize? It doesn't make sense."

"The past few months I've been going over my uncle's finances. Uncle Lenny was quite the player. Turns out, he owed money out his ass. Everybody came and collected on their debts. We were wiped out. Lauderdale pulled their account. Even your fuck-buddy Vanderdol bowed out," he smirked nastily. "The way things look, I'll have to sell the company so that my aunt doesn't end up totally screwed."

Dominique wanted to cry but she wouldn't give him the satisfaction. Arvind Thompson had turned out to be such an asshole. He must have been putting on quite the act in Memphis.

"I knew from day one what you were about," he went on to say. "I probably could have fucked you right on the desk that first day."

"What did I do to deserve this? Where is it coming from? It's almost as if you hate me or something."

"I don't hate you. But, I don't care too much for the likes of you. Women like you, Dominique, come a dime a dozen. They step in and out of men's lives not caring who they hurt. You remind me of my trifling mother. She did a number on my dad. She made him into the hateful man that he turned out to be. I now understand why he used to stomp her ass."

Dominique's head began spinning. She felt hot and clammy. She didn't want to hear anymore. A knot had formed in her chest. "Arvind, just go."

"Gladly. I know someone left an icebox where your heart used to be a long time ago."

Chapter Seventeen

Dominique's eyes were swollen shut from crying all night long. When Chad stopped by the next morning, he could immediately tell that something was wrong. He didn't say anything, just took her in his arms.

Once she was all cried out, he got up to get her a drink of water.

"You wanna talk about it?" She shook her head. "I think I know what's wrong. That metro-sexual nigga hurt you, didn't he?"

She looked at him with tear-rimmed eyes. "H-how did you know?"

"I been had his ass pegged the first time I saw him in the parkin' lot. Shit, he the type that thinks he's better than the res' of us. My money jus' as green as his fuckin' money."

"Speaking of money, I'm not going to have any soon. My position at the firm got cut," she told him with trembling lips.

"You ain't never gotta worry 'bout money, baby."

"Chad, we have a child on the way." She sniffed.

"The key term bein' we. It's our child. Together. And I'm gonna be a man and step up to the plate. But this time, I wanna do it right." To her astonishment, he got down on one knee. "Dominique, I know I'm ya second choice. I'm not all polished like Don Juan who left you heartbroken. But, I can promise you this: if you marry me, you'll never have to shed another fuckin' tear. Because I'ma treat ya ass like the queen that you are destined to be. You and my lil' shawty will be the two most important things in the world to me." He took her hand in his. "Will you be my wife?" He held up one finger. "Befo' you answer no, I jus' wanna say one mo' thing. I got a real job now- selling cell phones. I even went downtown and registered for the next session at the college."

"You did?" she asked, startled.

"And I'll cut out all them other women. I'm in this shit for the long haul. I messed up wit' my first baby mama, but she jus' wanted the bling-bling. You, I'm not gone even lie, you whipped me wit' that good ass pussy from day one. You got mad skills, baby." He chuckled but grew serious again. "I don't jus' love you for that, though. I love you for what's inside here." He pointed to her head. "And for what's inside there." He pointed to her heart.

"You love me?" she asked.

"Yeah. Why else you think a brotha be trippin' all the damn time?" He laughed and she even smiled a bit. "But on the serious tip, I want us to be a family. I won't ever leave you cryin', mama."

Sometimes you can't see the pearls because you're too busy searching for diamonds. Dominique realized that she'd had a true gem right before her eyes and had been over-looking him. Chad wasn't perfect, but he was willing to change. He was willing to work at becoming a better person, and that impressed the hell out of her.

When Dominique took Chad to meet her mother, it surprised her when the two of them hit it off. She had to admit to herself that maybe the problem didn't lie with Chad, but with her. She'd often times sought after the men who had high tech degrees and drove expensive cars. She'd looked to milk them out of whatever they were willing to give her. She'd enjoyed living like high society. Anything she'd wanted, she could make it happen by using her body. So, she'd used her body as often as it had taken.

She'd lost all sense of self, long before she'd began selling her soul to the highest bidder. She might not have prostituted her body literally but she considered herself no different than the women who walked the streets. They all had the same goal in mind: get that money, no matter what.

What her stepfather had done to her had a devastating affect on her self-image. She found that she'd closed off that part of her that could actually feel softer emotions. She'd done that to protect herself. When she'd finally allowed herself to let someone in, he'd hurt her to the core.

Yes, Arvind's ultimate rejection had hit her hard. He'd stepped into her life with cruel intentions. He'd been deceptive and mean.

Maybe he'd been hurt so much by what he thought his mother had done to his father that he took it out on all women.

When she looked back on it, maybe she hadn't been falling in love with him but with the idea of being in love. He'd presented a perfect package, making her think he was the man of her dreams He'd turned out to be her worst nightmare.

He'd been telling the truth about Troutman Mutual Funds & Investments. Once again she had been so wrong about yet another person, Mr. Troutman. He hadn't been the intelligent, respectful man that she'd thought he'd been. He'd been avoiding paying taxes, moving monies out of the business accounts for personal use, buying expensive cars and jewelry and charging it to the company's account. He'd been doing it all.

When Dominique had finally pulled herself together, she'd gone to collect her personal belongings. Thankfully, Arvind hadn't been anywhere around. Brenda had been there, packing all of her stuff up as well.

"It's so hard to start all over again," she'd said. Her eyes were red from crying. "I'm out of a job and it's close to the holidays. With no job, that means no insurance. I have a son with asthma. I've got to get something soon."

"You'll find something Brenda. You're an excellent Administrative Assistant. We'll all find something." She pulled the numerous awards that she'd received off the wall and took pictures off her desk and put them into a box. "So, do you know who's taking over the company?"

"David Savkovic."

"David?"

"Yes. You know his parents are filthy rich. They loaned him what he needed without batting an eye."

Dominique knew that she might as well keep on packing. No way would she ask David for a job position. The way he felt about her, he'd probably place her in the maintenance department.

Just as she was getting the last of her things, David walked into the office.

"Miss Green, don't be so quick to leave. I have a proposition for you."

Dominique shook her head. Not again. She'd grown tired of using her body to get ahead. She wouldn't do it anymore. Besides, she had to think about her unborn child now.

"No propositions, David. The woman that you used to know, you won't find her in me anymore," she said quietly.

"I know. Lauretta pretty much gave me the 411 on what happened between you and Arvind Thompson. What a snake." She stared at him in surprise. He thought that about Arvind? Maybe there was still hope. "And I know all about your condition, too. With a new addition to the family, you're going to need medical coverage. So, I have a *business* proposition for you," he said.

"David, with our history, do you think that would be wise? The rumors will fly."

"I don't give a damn about rumors. I own a multi-million dollar company." He smiled. "But, seriously. I don't know anything about being a CEO. Hell, I'm content to just remain in New Accounts as a supervisor, even though that's not possible. Regardless of what happened in the past, you're the best woman for the job."

"Best woman for the job? What job?"

"I'd like you to be the new CEO. You know this place like the back of your hand. I know that you and Mr. Troutman worked side by side. You're a go-getter and you have strength and determination." He walked over to her desk and picked up the box of her personal items. "I'll be taking this to your new office."

Dominique felt tears form in her eyes. "But, why are you doing this for me after how I treated you?"

"Because, I know how hard it is for a black woman in the business world to get ahead. You did what you had to do. You didn't use me, Dominique. I allowed myself to be used," he admitted. "So, there are no hard feelings. Let's put the past behind us."

She got all choked up. "Thank you," she managed to get past her tight throat.

"Well, I think you should get Brenda and let her know that she's got a new title, Account Executive."

"Who'll replace Brenda?"

"Lauretta Smith, of course."

"David, you are an angel."

"Only in your dream." He gave her a wink and left to take her personal stuff to her new office.

Epilogue

Chad and Dominique's marriage turned out to be one of Tampa's most extravagant affairs. It took place at the Church Without Walls. She looked so beautiful in her flowing, white gown. Lauretta had stood in as her Matron of Honor.

Chad, extremely handsome outside of his street wear, beamed from ear to ear. He finally had his woman. Even though it had taken trickery to get her, he knew that only patience and love could keep her. He vowed to treasure her for the rest of their lives. He felt that she deserved it, especially after what she'd revealed about her stepfather. With him by her side, no one would ever hurt her again. He'd swear that on his mother's grave.

His mother just so happened to like Dominique. That damn sure was a first because she couldn't stand his baby mama. At least he wouldn't have to worry about banning her from their home because he would have if she'd tripped about the woman who had his heart.

They rented out one of the rooms in The Regency for the reception. The room had been decorated beautifully. All the food had been catered. Chad had suggested a bartender, who served mixed drinks. They'd even brought in a live D J. They laughed, danced, ate and had such a good time. When it came time to throw the bride's bouquet Lauretta damn near knocked over one of the bridesmaids in order to catch it.

Their wedding night was perfect. Chad undressed his new wife and stared at her like she was the most beautiful woman in the world. He couldn't stop smiling like he'd won an Olympic trophy.

"Damn, I love you." he stated.

"I love you too." She stared into his eyes and realized that she truly meant it.

"It's kinda hard for me to believe this shit." He shook his head. "You're my wife."

"You'd better believe it." She kissed him square on the lips and he welcomed her tongue in his mouth. It was ironic how everything had turned out. She'd thought that Arvind would be the man she'd be uncrossing her legs for every night, but it had turned out to be Chad.

THE END

DEAR READER,

I hope you enjoyed *Uncrossing Her Legs*. If so, I would appreciate it if you would help others enjoy this book too.

Review it. Tell other readers why you liked this book by reviewing it on Amazon, Barnes & Noble, Kobo, Smashwords or whichever website from which you purchased it.

Recommend it. Help other readers find this book by recommending it to your Facebook friends, Twitter followers, readers' groups and discussions boards.

Lend it. This eBook is lending enabled, so please, share it with a friend.

e-Gift it. eBooks make perfect gifts for avid readers!

P.S. I love to hear from my readers. Please connect with me online.

Novels
1. Big Tobe: Retribution
2. Ex-boyfriend
3. Fetish
4. Food Stamp Bitches
5. Headlines
6. In Need of a Joshua Man
7. Panzina's Passion
8. Project Queen
9. Project Queen 2
10. Real Hood Wives of St. Pete., The
11. Spin Cycle
12. They Call Me Mr. G-Spot
13. Uncrossing Her Legs
14. Unpretty Secrets
15. What About Your Friends
16. When There Are No Tomorrows

Novellas
17. My Cousin, Lenore
18. Under the Oak Tree
19. Unseen Wounds

Young Adult Titles
20. Janell Has an Attitude
21. Sequoia Denise, Just a Kid

Short Stories
22. Boy Who Needed Someone & Other Stories, The
23. Christmas Morning
24. Daddy Never Loved Me

25. How Many Licks
26. Other Crap...
27. Party in Wo... a T...
28. She Gets Wh... She Wants

Boxed Sets
29. Hot Urban...
30. Hot Urban Fiction...
31. Hot Urban Fiction on My...
32. Project Queen Collec...
33. Whatever It Is... Comes O...

25. How Many Licks
26. Office Grapevine
27. Power in Words, The
28. She Gets What She Wants

Boxed Sets
29. Hot Urban Fiction Mix 1
30. Hot Urban Fiction Mix 2
31. Hot Urban Fiction Mix 3
32. Project Queen Collection
33. Project Queen/Big Tobe Collection
34. Whatever Teen Series Collection

ABOUT THE AUTHOR

Teresa D. Patterson is the author of several novels, novellas and short stories. She is the founder of Edit Again Publications and has a degree in business.

To find out more information about the author, for book orders, and/or to read book excerpts, please visit her website: teresadpatterson.net

You may also join her on Facebook, Twitter and Blogspot.

CONNECT WITH THE AUTHOR

Twitter:
https:/twitter.com/teresapatterson

Facebook:
www.facebook.com/teresadiannapatterson

Blogspot:
http://teresadpatterson.blogspot.com

Pinterest:
http://pinterest.com/TeeRee1

Email:
teresadpatterson2004@yahoo.com

EXCERPT FROM

Spin Cycle

BY TERESA D. PATTERSON

PROLOGUE

P rincipal Austin Johnson monitored the hallway as the students filed into the school building, rushing toward their lockers and classrooms. He was a tall, handsome, light-complexioned brother, with a smooth skin tone. He stood six-feet four, wearing a three-pieced suit and tie. His broad shoulders and muscular physique were hidden underneath the suit, but he wore it well.

"Slow it down, Johnny Ridgecrest. Don't make me send you to the office to get a detention for running in the hallways. You shouldn't have been macking with the girls in the bus circle. You wouldn't be late getting to class," he called out causing the young teen to blush in embarrassment.

"Awww man, Mr. Johnson. Why you gotta put me on blast?" Johnny mumbled good-naturedly, hurrying past the principal.

"Destiny. Destiny. Stopping slamming that locker door before someone's hand gets smashed in it. Get to class. Children, the warning bell has rang, you have thirty seconds to get to class. I need these hallways cleared in thirty seconds," he bellowed. The children scattered, giggling as they did so.

Austin watched as a stray student with big-framed glasses, rushed past shooting him a nervous glance. He wore a huge backpack and struggled to stand up straight with the weight of it.

"Why are you giving me that guilty look?" Mr. Johnson asked. "Yes, you're late."

"No fair. My bus just got here," the student whined. "And I didn't even have a chance to go to my locker yet. And I just bet I'm not going to be able to open that combination lock on the first try. Drats!"

"Okay. Okay," Austin said, waving him off. "Go to the front office to get a pass so you won't be marked tardy by your teacher."

"Thanks, Mr. Johnson," the boy said gratefully and shuffled off down the hallway. Austin smiled and shook his head.

Another hectic week had just begun at Thurgood Marshall Middle School. As he headed toward his office, he spotted Mrs. Greta Stevenson entering the building. He rushed to hold the door open for her.

"Thank you, Dr. Johnson," she said. "Good morning."

"Good morning, Mrs. Stevenson," he greeted. She smiled and breezed past him. He caught a scent of the soft fragrance she wore. For some reason, he turned around. That's when he saw another teacher, Larry Newsome, watching Greta.

He knew that look. It was one of lust and longing. It was a predatory gaze, and it unnerved him.

Larry must have felt Austin's eyes burning into him because he glanced in his direction. Knowing that he'd been caught gawking at Mrs. Stevenson's ass didn't embarrass him in the least. He nodded his head in the direction of the principal and walked off.

I already don't like him, Austin thought. *He gives me a bad vibe.*

Chapter One

Greta Stevenson groaned as she reluctantly pushed herself into a sitting position on the couch. She wanted to continue lounging, but the three baskets of dirty laundry glared at her. She wished she could wave a magic wand and make them float outside and into the trunk of her car.

Those liars, she fumed. *They told me my shit would be working last Tuesday. Now, here it is damn near two weeks later and my washer and dryer are still on the blink. That's why I detest living in apartment complexes. The trifling maintenance personnel never fix jack. And when they do—the crap still doesn't work.*

She couldn't wait until she signed the lease on her four-bedroom home in south Saint Petersburg. Her new house would be located on Pinellas Point Drive, known as *The Point.* Quite a few of the famed and the elite purchased homes in that area. She'd worked hard to earn her bread and butter and finally it all seemed worth it. She looked forward to leaving the apartment behind that she'd shared with her deceased husband, Gerald, and start anew.

She sighed as she picked up one of the baskets of clothes. Thinking about Gerald always brought about a melancholy mood because it reminded her of the letter and the pictures.

I wouldn't go there. I won't think about it. He's gone and I just need to get him out of my head forever. But how?

She blinked back the tears and shook Gerald out of her memory and concentrated on something else.

She was tired. She didn't get home from work until almost seven that evening. She had to play taxi cab driver for two of her students. Their trifling parents hadn't bothered to show up to get them after detention ended. That wasn't right. She couldn't understand why some people didn't just burn their damn tubes and not have children. Everyone wasn't cut out to be parents.

She couldn't stand smart-alecky kids who didn't know the meaning of the word respect. However, she didn't fault the child. She blamed the parent for not teaching them manners.

Greta had been teaching for fifteen years and her nerves were at the breaking point. She had just about enough of dealing with other people's demon seed. It might be time for a career change.

Take today, for instance, she had to stay late because two want-to-be-thugs thought it was cute to practice rolling blunts with their notebook paper the previous week. That type of behavior would not be tolerated in her classroom. She sent a letter home to their parents and received no response. She followed up with a phone call. One of the boy's mothers had been downright rude. She gave Greta a piece of her mind for disturbing her. She pretty much stated that she could care less about her child's behavior. Her exact words had been: *I don't give a fuck about what he does at school, as long as he doesn't do it at home.*

Speaking to the other boy's father had been like having a conversation with Forest Gump. The brother had been off in the ozone layer or something. He kept inhaling and coughing making her think that he might be smoking through the phone.

She had no choice but to assign the two children an after school detention, hoping that would convince them of their wrong-doing. Hence, the reason she arrived home late. Neither of the boy's parents came to pick them up. She ended up taking them home. She simply refused to let them walk and felt it was her responsibility to make sure they arrived at their doorsteps safely.

Greta took the first basket of clothes to the car and placed them in the trunk. Today hadn't been any better. The incident with the two boys was actually mild in comparison. She shook her head as she thought about it.

She'd encountered a little foul-mouthed heifer that made her blood pressure rise. Little *Miss I'm America's Next Top Model* came to school with her breasts on display. When Greta advised her to put on a jacket, *Miss Too Grown for My Own Good* got an attitude and told Greta to kiss her ass.

Greta was known for being a no-nonsense type of teacher that didn't take crap off the children. That's how she'd persevered for so many years. You had to have patience, guts and a backbone to be around hardheaded, wayward teens all day, damn near every day, for so long. Not too many of her students tried her because they knew that she didn't play the radio when it came to her classroom.

For some reason, *Miss Pumps and a Bump* stepped over the boundaries. Greta had to count to ten and it took the patience of Job to hold herself back. She almost came across her desk and rolled the girl's head around like she was on *the Exorcist.*

The new principal just so happened to be sitting in the classroom that morning and sent the *Stripper in Training* to the office. It was a good thing, too, because Greta would have probably lost her job and caught a charge on the same day if he hadn't intervened. She'd never been disrespected in such a manner in all her years of teaching.

Greta finished putting the last basket of clothes into the car and shut the trunk. She wasn't looking forward to the visit to the

Laundromat up the street. Some unsavory characters hung around the facility. Since it was opened twenty-four seven, the homeless saw fit to loiter there. Most of the time, they just begged for spare change. Even though they were probably harmless, Greta couldn't let her guard down because she'd heard of reported rapes and muggings in the area.

Surprisingly, when she pulled up, she found the place empty.

Good. I won't have to keep looking over my shoulder, she thought. It was semi-dark, and a single woman always had to be cautious. She popped the trunk and took the clothes inside.

After she had arrived home, took a shower, and cooked dinner, she sorted the clothes. If only she'd gotten home earlier, she'd be done with the laundry by now. A dusty, white, clock on the wall ticked. It was eight thirty. It should take her no more than an hour and a half, two hours tops to wash and dry all of her clothes. She threw them into vacant washing machines, poured in detergent, and added coins to begin the wash cycle.

The washing machines hummed and she sat down and began grading papers. Minutes later, she heard someone enter, but didn't look up, assuming it was a vagrant.

Damn. There goes my concentration.

"Mrs. Stevenson, fancy seeing you here," someone called out. She looked up into the handsome face of Principal Austin Johnson.

"Hello, Dr. Johnson," she greeted politely. She saw him struggling to pull a large container of clothes inside. She put her folders on the seat next to her and went over to hold the door open for him.

"Thank you," he said, graciously.

"No problem. So, what brings you here?" she asked.

"I guess the same thing that brings you here," he replied, pointing at his clothes. "Dirty laundry." The two chuckled.

Greta returned to her seat, discreetly surveying Mr. Johnson as he went about the business of putting his clothes into the washing machines.

Mr. Johnson was the new principal of the middle school where she taught. She didn't really know much about him, just what she'd heard. He'd graduated from Northeast High School, enlisted in the Army, serving a four year term. He returned to St. Petersburg to teach children. He'd been a juvenile justice counselor, a teacher at the recreational center, an assistant principal at one of the elementary schools, and now he was the principal of the middle school.

She heard that he'd been married, but was presently divorced. She wondered if he were dating anybody. She watched as he poured entirely too much detergent into the machine.

She thought, *a man that fine should not be doing his own laundry. I'd hand wash his drawers. Damn.*

Austin glanced her way and their eyes locked. Greta swallowed.

Hell, I hope he can't read my thoughts. Shoot, then again, I hope he can.

"So, you almost went postal on that kid today, huh?" he said, smiling as he closed the lid on the washer. He had perfect white teeth and dimples. Standing at about six feet four, he was a tall refreshing drink of water. Greta's throat suddenly became parched.

"At times, it gets hard to brace myself. But, I'd never put a hand on a student," she answered.

"Sure you wouldn't. I know you envision shaking one of 'em like a bobble headed doll, though," he joked. "I have those moments," he admitted. "Especially being the new principal of a fundamental school. Whew," he exhaled.

"I can't even begin to feel your pain, brother," she sympathized.

She got up to check her clothes. They'd stopped so she began taking them out of the machine.

After she'd gotten out of the shower earlier she'd thrown on one of her hoochie mama skirts. Just because she was a teacher didn't mean she had to dress like a nun when she was home.

As she bent over, unknown to her, the cheerleader skirt rose in the back. That captured Mr. Johnson's attention.

"Um-" He cleared his throat. "You know, red is my favorite color."

"Excuse me?" she quipped, turning to stare at him innocently.

"I said, red is my favorite color," he repeated. "You're wearing the hell out of them thongs," he boldly stated. "You're about to make a brother burst at the seams."

"Dr. Johnson." Greta blushed. "I am so sorry. I had no idea." She straightened up immediately, pulling self-consciously at the skirt's hem.

The thought that he'd been drooling at her ass cheeks turned her on. Hell, she knew that her body was together. She worked out three nights a week to keep everything toned to perfection. She wasn't about to the let the fact that she was pushing up on forty keep her from feeling and being sexy. If the truth were told, she looked better now than she had when she was in her mid-twenties. She had rock hard abs, a slim twenty-four inch waist, a banging set of tits and a tight ass. To top it off, she was easy on the eyes.

Her mocha colored skin was flawless and make-up free. She had a set of Angelina Jolie type lips that made a brother think dirty thoughts.

Her attractiveness and attributes did not go unnoticed by Austin. She had nice, shapely legs. They looked well-toned in the short skirt she sported. Her smooth brown skin glowed, appearing inviting. He wanted to touch her to find out if she was as soft as she appeared to be.

As Greta went to put her laundry into dryers, he watched. He willed her to bend over and show that red thong one more time. His member grew harder than a slab of concrete, the imprint straining against the front of his pants, as he thought about it.

Since he'd made the comment about her panties, she wouldn't look his way. Austin hadn't played the aggressive role in a minute. He didn't have to. Women threw themselves at him on a regular basis. Even some of the teachers, the ones who got paid to teach the future generation, were nothing but sluts. That's how he ended up divorced. He'd been too worn out from screwing all the teachers, and hadn't been able to get it up for his wife. That got old and she left him. He wasn't mad at her though. If the roles had been reversed, he would have done the same thing.

Mrs. Stevenson, he couldn't quite figure her out. He'd been at the new school for almost three months and she hadn't given him a second glance. He'd pulled her file and did some research. He couldn't complain about her track record as a teacher. She was excellent in her field and he could tell she genuinely cared about the children. He saw it in her interactions with them in the hallway and from the glimpse he'd gotten sitting in her classroom.

She wasn't married. As far as he knew, she didn't have a man in her life.

So, what's the deal? He wondered. He hoped she *did* like men. Was that it? Maybe she liked fish instead of beef.

He would find out. If she swayed the other way, that was her prerogative. It would just be a damned shame for all that fineness to be wasted like that, though.

He stood up to check the washer then he turned toward her, breaking the silence. "If I offended you, I apologize," he said.

Greta had her back turned, attempting to compose herself. She didn't know why she was being betrayed by her body. Her swollen nipples strained against the thin blouse she wore as she pictured the two of them in some uncompromising positions. She bit the corner of her lip.

She had to control her emotions. She'd never before contemplated doing something so wild and reckless, but she wanted to let him ravish her. She needed to feel him buried deep inside her.

Her stomach churned at the thoughts. She turned toward him and smiled, pretending that he had no affect on her.

"I don't get easily offended," she said. Her traitorous eyes fell on his crotch. "Let's just cut the bullshit, okay? I don't mince my words. I say what I mean and mean what I say. What about you?"

Her heated gaze made his dick jump.

So, she's a dick bandit after all.

"I'm pretty much straight forward," he answered.

"You want to fuck me, don't you?" she asked.

"Hell yes. Now, that's what I'm talking about."

"As long as it doesn't get out, I'm down with it. But, I want to make one thing clear: I don't mix business with pleasure." She looked him straight in the eye. "This will be a one-time occurrence. Got that?"

What the fuck ever.

He called the shots. If he wanted another piece of ass after he'd test driven it, he'd get another piece. "Yeah, if that's the way you want it," he said, unblinking.

Greta stared as the bulge in the front of his pants grew. It rose and stirred like a trapped anaconda. The right choice to make would be releasing the beast. She reached for his zipper and slowly tugged it down.

The head of his large dick sprang forward, leaping at Greta like a jack-in-the-box. She charmed the rest of the snake out, stroking as she watched it grow. It was long and beautiful, having both depth and width. Just the sight of it made her mouth water. However, she wasn't going there, not with him. The brother could get his dick sucked by someone else. It wasn't like he couldn't find a number of women to do it.

She would show Principal Johnson that she wasn't about playing games. If he wanted to fuck, that's what she would do. No extra side items were on the menu, just pure pussy.

"My place is right around the corner. You can either follow me in your car, or we can take mine. I'll drop you back off," she suggested, continuing to stroke him with one hand as she spoke.

A moan escaped his lips. He was close to popping and didn't want to wait. He looked her over suggestively. "What's wrong with right here?"

"You mean, in the Laundromat? Where anyone can walk in? I don't know-"

Before she could finish the sentence, he lifted her up onto one of the washing machines. "Learn to step outside the box, Mrs. Stevenson. Spontaneity will keep a man coming back."

Greta could feel the motion of the machine as it switched to the spin cycle. When it began swirling around, the whole machine trembled. Austin spread her legs apart. The little skirt she wore allowed easy access. He wasted no time, pulling her panties to the side and easing into her.

She inhaled from the first feel of him. She felt stretched to the max; it had been so long. He continued to stroke in and out until she loosened up. She moaned and gripped the coin slot on the machine and held on for life. As the machine bounced, she bounced. The more she bounced the deeper he plunged.

"Oh, Dr. Johnson," she screamed, feeling her muscles clench and unclench. "I'm coming. I'm coming."

"Mrs. Stevenson," he answered. He could feel her vaginal muscles pulsating and contracting. She was so wet and tight it amazed him. He bucked harder.

She felt delirious and couldn't control the words that flew out of her mouth. "Dr. Johnson, fuck this pussy. Fuck it. Fuck it. Fuck it," she chanted.

"You want me to beat it up? Huh? I'll beat that pussy up real good. Turn that fine ass around," he commanded.

Greta didn't know how she ended up on a folding table, but she was beyond caring. All she knew was that she'd been craving sex for a long time, and now she was getting what she needed.

As he pounded her from the back, he grabbed a hand full of her hair and pulled.

"Damn. That shit feels so good," she said. She'd never had a man pull her hair. Chills raced through her entire body.

"I'mma wax this ass," he panted.

"Wax it."

She threw her ass back at him. He plunged into her. She paused just momentarily and clenched her vaginal muscles. Then she released them. She continued to do that until she had him just where she wanted him. She milked him until he couldn't do anything but scream.

"Shit." He throbbed then spurted like a volcano. She could feel the hotness of his jism inside her.

Gteta wanted to climax again so badly that her stomach muscles ached. She wrapped her legs around his waist, trying to keep him inside her.

Austin pulled out. He was trying to call the shots. She knew that game. Even as her thigh muscles trembled from restraint, she wouldn't give him the upper hand.

He adjusted his trousers as he stood back and stared at her in satisfaction. "Mrs. Stevenson, you've made it to the top of the Principal's list. You get straight A's." He smiled cockily, zipped up his pants and turned to watch as Greta fixed her clothes. Even though she had been a real good lay, there was something different about her. He knew he'd definitely be getting into those panties again. He'd purposefully pushed her to the edge, but pulled back right when she'd been close to gushing.

He knew women hated that, but it worked. She could act like she didn't know what time it was, but *he* was the keeper of the time clock. He and Mrs. Stevenson would meet up again for round two. He just had to play his cards right.

Chapter Two

Greta returned home and hopped into the shower again. Her emotions were charged and she was filled with such energy. As she lathered her body with shower gel, she thought about Austin's hands touching her, his dick filling her, him pulling her hair. She wanted him again with a passion she'd never experienced before.

Even though she felt a sense of satisfaction, she also felt used. Austin straight up dissed her once he'd gotten his rocks off. That smart ass comment about her making the Principal's list pissed her off. She'd told him that having sex with him would be a one-time occurrence, and she meant that. A man like Austin Johnson could make her lose her head, and that was the last thing she needed to do. *Didn't you already lose your head? I mean, you only fucked the principal of your middle school in the Laundromat.*

She shivered as she remembered, closing her eyes to recapture those few minutes she'd felt close to heaven. She hadn't felt so alive in years. Buying that red thong and bra set at Victoria Secrets had been worth the money.

Once she'd gotten dressed for bed, she set about putting the clean laundry away. She hung shirts and pants on hangers in the closet and folded the shorts, panties, bras, and tee-shirts, tucking them away in a drawer.

She tried to clear her mind of all thoughts of Mr. Johnson. She'd just as soon forget anyway. The man was off limits. He was the principal of the school where she worked, for Pete's sake.

She couldn't believe she'd let her hormones get the best of her. She'd acted like a horny teenager on prom night. She didn't know how she would be able to look Mr. Johnson in the eye after their heated encounter.

Damn, the sex had been off the chain. She hadn't been pounded like that in years. She'd been experiencing a dry spell so long that it had been almost turned into a draught. She'd needed that stress relief.

But, did she have to do it in a Laundromat ...and with the principal? A bitch was acting like she hadn't been raised right. She had turned into a low moral skank because the sight of her panties turned a man on.

She heard her great grandmother's voice inside her head.

Satan, that's what it is. That's just the devil. Plain and simple.

She was weak in the flesh. She'd have to go to church on Sunday just to purge herself. Hell, after what she'd let happen, they needed to pull out the holy water and the crucifix, maybe even lay hands on her.

"What the hell was I thinking?" she wondered aloud. "It won't happen again." But the tingling in her lower extremities from just thinking about Austin said otherwise.

Her cell phone beeped three times indicating that she had a text message. She picked it up.

Mrs. Stevenson, will you please meet me in my office first thing in the morning? She read. It was from Principal Johnson. What the hell was he up to? Hadn't she told him that what happened between them wouldn't happen again? She'd be damned if she showed up.

The phone beeped again.

Don't even think about not showing up, it read. She sighed. Tomorrow would be a long day.

Greta had just gotten deeply engrossed in a book written by Chamsil. She was damn near about to touch herself under the covers when her home phone rang.

"Shit," she swore, putting the book aside and grabbing the cordless. "This had better not be a damn booty call," she snapped. All of her acquaintances knew she didn't accept any calls of that nature.

"Calm down, Miss Lady. I just wanted to holla at you. You are one hard person to catch up with. I stopped by your apartment, but you weren't there." It was Larry, one of her co-workers, another teacher.

"I had to go do laundry," she said.

"Oh, really? They still didn't fix your shit, huh?"

"Hell no and I'm about ready to tell them motherfuckers about themselves. This shit is ridiculous."

"I feel you."

"So, what are you up to Larry?"

"I just finished grading some papers. Half my students don't know simple math. What the fuck kind of shit is that?"

"They'd rather be parked in front of a PlayStation or watching music videos instead of studying math," she said.

"I know that's right," he agreed. "Hey, I've been meaning to ask you, what's your take on our new principal?"

Greta damn near dropped the phone. "U-Um, he's nice, I guess," she managed to say. "What about you?"

"I think he's a sneaky motherfucker. But, that's just my opinion."

"Larry, do I detect a hint of jealousy?" she asked.

"Hell to the nah. Personally, I think I got the brother beat. I mean, I'm a handsome ass motherfucker. Shit, I got abs and arms that would make Dwayne Johnson jealous. Granted, I don't drive a sporty ass BMW like Mr. Johnson, but I got a nice whip. He gets drawers thrown at him daily, but so do I."

Greta laughed. "You are a mess. Is that all you think about every day? You're supposed to be teaching, remember?"

"I do teach. I teach math all day to my students. But, at night, it's Love Making 101. You need to sign up for the class." He laughed through the phone.

"Larry, you already know how I feel about mixing business with pleasure."

"Yeah, I know," he said dryly.

"Well, I'm going to turn in, Larry. I have to meet Mr. Johnson in his office early in the morning."

"What do that nigga want?" he asked suspiciously.

"I have no idea," she answered truthfully.

"Well, be careful. I heard that he's already had a few teachers bent over that desk," he half-joked. "But, I know you can handle your business."

"Good night, Larry," she said pretending to ignore the last part of his statement.

"Good night."

For some reason the thought of another teacher bent over Mr. Johnson's desk annoyed her. She shook the thought and picked the book she'd been reading back up. However, her concentration was broken and all she could think of was riding Austin's dick like a thoroughbred.

The next morning, Greta took a while choosing an outfit to wear. She finally dressed professionally in a two pieced, pinstriped pants suit. If Mr. Johnson tried to get at her stuff again, he'd have barriers to get through. She wasn't giving in easily, even if she did want to.

She arrived at the school at little after seven o'clock. That would give them plenty of time to discuss whatever he had to talk about. The children weren't supposed to arrive on the school's grounds until 8:15 AM, but she saw a few already sitting out front.

"Good morning," she greeted. She always made it a point to speak to every child she encountered. You never knew just how much a smile or a kind word could make a child's day.

"Hey, Mrs. Stevenson." She recognized Jamisha, the student that dressed inappropriately and came out the mouth wrong with her the day before. An older woman with a two-toned hairdo stood next to her, frowning deeply.

Lord, please don't let my morning start off with a ghetto-style brawl, she prayed silently. She didn't want to come up out her high heels and use one. But, she would if she had to. She surveyed the other semi-large woman. She could probably take her down. Most ghetto chicks were all talk and no action anyway.

"Hi, Jamisha. How are you, this morning?" Jamisha rolled her eyes. "And how are you?" she greeted the woman.

"I'm jus' fine. I'm Ms. Bethune. Jamisha's mama. Now, Misha tells me dat you sent her out ya class 'cause of what she was wearin' yesterday. I wanna know what she had on."

"I already told you, Mama," Jamisha whined.

"Shut ya mouth girl. I am talkin' to ya teacher," Ms. Bethune hissed.

"Well, she was wearing a half shirt. The school's policy informs that tank tops or half shirts aren't allowed. Had she put on a jacket, as I suggested, I wouldn't have sent her out of the classroom. It's just that, wearing something so revealing can be distracting to the other students," she explained to the obviously irate woman who glared at her.

The woman's neck turned so fast Gerta thought she might have caused whiplash. "A fuckin' half shirt?" she yelled at her daughter. "What da fuck you come up in school wearin' some shit like dat fuh?" The mama chastised.

"Mama, I'll wear whatever I wanna wear."

"See, you lucky dis teacher standin' here. 'Cause if she wasn't, I'd beat ya ass down where you stand. I ain't raisin' no damn tramp. You supposed to wear the clothes that I buy fuh ya ass. I didn't buy no fuckin' half shirts."

"I didn't say you did." Jamisha sucked air through her teeth and rolled her eyes again.

"Gurl." Ms. Bethune drew back her hand and that's when Greta felt it was best to intervene.

"Ms. Bethune, don't." She quickly stepped between mother and daughter. "Obviously there's a communication break down between yourself and your daughter. However, getting upset in public is never a good idea. Perhaps it's best that you discuss this private matter at home," she suggested.

"Ain't nothin' to discuss. She gonna do what da fuck I say do. She gonna go to school to learn and not to pick up nasty ass boys. All dey want is what's between ya legs anyways." She pushed her daughter's forehand with her index finger.

"Mama."

"Don't mama me. Shit, how da hell you think I got five kids now? Men tell one lie afta a fuckin' nother one to get ya stuff. You don't wanna have no kid. Raisin' kids ain't no damn joke. I'm tryin' to keep you from goin' thru the shit I go through erry day."

"You don't go through nothin'. I'm the one got to babysit all the time," Jamisha grumbled. "Besides, I ain't even doin' nothin'," she griped.

"And you won't if I can help it. You got me comin' up here all upset, 'bout to go off on dis lady and all she tryin' to do is tell you right from wrong." She turned an apologetic look toward Greta. "My bad ma'am. Dis gurl is jus' fast. Thank God the res' of my kids is boys."

Greta smiled slightly. She couldn't fathom having five kids. Hell, she didn't think she'd ever have that many unless she pushed out quintuplets.

"Ms. Bethune, I understand your concern. However, Jamisha is one of my most promising students." Greta could see the girl's eyes light up and the angry look left her face. "Do you know that she scored the highest in the whole classroom on the FCAT test in reading?"

"Nah, I didn't know dat. Is dat so?" Her face seemed to lose some of its irritation.

"Yes, it certainly is. Jamisha is also an incredible writer. She's extremely talented."

"I knew she liked to write and thangs. She always readin' too. I jus' don't like huh choice of books. Zane. Dat woman is too graphic. No teenager ain't got no business readin' dat. Now, myself, I like readin' some Eric Jerome Dickey."

"Really?"

"Yep. Sho nuff. I buy erry one of his books. He sho nuff can write for a man, and he is fine too." Her eyes narrowed as though she saw something she wanted really badly. "But not half as fine as dat nigga comin' dis way." She put her hands on her hip and just gawked. Girlfriend didn't have any shame in her game.

Greta turned in the direction of Ms. Bethune's gaze. Principal Johnson. For a second her heart rate increased. She quickly composed herself.

"Good morning Principal Johnson," she said calmly as he approached.

"Good morning, ladies. How are you this fine morning?" The man was pure charismatic. It was plain to see that Ms. Bethune was smitten.

"You're the principal?" Her eyes said, "*Damn.*"

"Yes, I am. And you are?"

"I'm Brenda Bethune, Jamisha's mother." The woman extended a hand with long acrylic nails. Of all designs, she had President Obama and his wife on the thumbs. Now, if that didn't take the cake, Greta didn't know what did.

Damn, look at how fast that bitch switched from ghetto queen to sophisticated lady, Greta thought dryly.

"I'm pleased to meet you." Austin threw her a dazzling smile that enhanced his dimples.

"The pleasure is all mine," Ms. Bethune drooled. "I was just speaking with Miss – er, I didn't get your name."

"Stevenson. Mrs. Stevenson," she answered with a tight smile.

"I was just speaking with Mrs. Stevenson regarding Jamisha's behavior yesterday. She was out of line and it definitely will not happen again. You have my word on that."

"I'm happy to hear that Ms. Bethune. It takes a village." He threw out the cliché with another dazzling smile.

"Well, I have to get to work. If there are any further problems, don't hesitate to call me." She stared directly at Mr. Johnson when she said the last part.

"You have a good day ma'am." He was just eating up the attention while Greta silently burned with annoyance.

"You too," she purred. "Oh, and you too," she added for Greta's sake.

Bitch please.

"You do the same." Greta wanted to roll her eyes, but she just smiled sweetly.

"Mrs. Stevenson, I'll be ready to meet with you in a minute. If you want, you can wait for me in my office. I have to make my rounds," Austin said.

He showed no indication that he had anything but business on his mind. It was as though yesterday evening had never occurred. For some reason, Greta felt slightly disappointed.

"I'll put on the coffee," she said, walking off briskly.

It was 8:20 when Principal Johnson entered the office. Greta had made the coffee and was sipping from a cup of the hot steamy liquid she held in her hands.

"Good morning again, Mrs. Stevenson," he said, depositing his fine frame behind the desk. "I have a proposition for you," he leaned toward her and she noticed the gleam in his beautiful unusually gray eyes.

"Here we go," she mumbled under her breath.

"I've been checking you out for quite some time."

Is this bitch a stalker?

"I see that you've been teaching for fifteen years. That's quite a while."

What? Did I miss something?

"Um...teaching?" she asked, hesitantly.

"Yes, you've been a teacher for fifteen years, right?"

"Oh, yes. Yes. I have."

So, where is he going with this?

"That's remarkable. It requires strength and dedication. You obviously have both."

"This really *is* a business meeting?" The question was out of her mouth before she could stop it.

Mr. Johnson smirked. "What did you think it would be? Contrary to popular belief, I don't bend women over my desk on the state's time. I have a job to do and that's what I aim to do. This school is suffering and I'm going to make sure that there's a noticeable improvement in the upcoming months. I don't play when it comes to children and education." He lifted a file from his desk. "And from what I've read, you don't either. That's why I have an offer for you."

Now Greta's interest was peaked. "What type of an offer?"

"Unfortunately, Mrs. Niles will no longer be the assistant principal, for reasons I don't care to disclose at this moment. She'll be leaving at the end of this month. Therefore, there will be a vacancy." He paused and stared at her intensely. "I'd like for you to fill it."

Greta's mouth dropped. Surprise couldn't even describe what she felt. This was totally unexpected.

"Ma'am, you may want to close your mouth. We wouldn't want a fly to land in there," he joked.

She cleared her throat. It took a minute to pull it together. But, it wasn't long before she was once again the professional, debonair woman who radiated confidence.

"Mr. Johnson, I appreciate your offer. I'll think it over and get back with you. When do you need a decision?"

"I was pushing for one by the next PSTA meeting. That will give you two weeks time."

"Thank you. I'm sure I'll be able to let you know something before then," she said politely.

"Thank you for your time, Mrs. Stevenson."

"You're welcome." Their eyes met and she was the first to look away. She cleared her throat. "Well, if that's all, I'll be heading to the classroom."

"Yes, that's all I can think of." She got up to leave. He waited until she made it to the door. "Oh— Mrs. Stevenson?" She turned just in time to catch the glint in his eyes. "Thanks for last night," he said mischievously. "I'll never dread doing laundry again." He gave her a half-smile, half-smirk.

She stared at his desk picturing the two of them on it. Having him bend her over that desk wasn't such a bad idea. As a matter-of-fact, it was quite appealing. She blushed and quickly left his office before she ended up making a fool of herself.

Chapter Three

Greta sat grading papers. She wanted to be finished by nine o'clock because *Criminal Minds* which featured that fine actor, Shemar Moore would be coming on. She knew there was no chance in hell of her ever meeting the man, but every opportunity she got she drooled over him like a damn groupie.

Of course her phone had to ring and break her concentration. It seemed like every time she got busy, it rang off the hook.

"Hello?"

"Hey Girl. What you doin'?" It was Cindy, her oldest and dearest friend. Cindy was a straight up trip and she always enjoyed talking with her.

"Grading papers. What else."

"Girl, why don't you throw them damn papers to the side and hang out wit' me tonight?"

"Hang out where? Child, now you know I don't set foot in these ghetto-fied, dirty foot clubs in St. Pete."

"Are you implyin' that I do, skank? "

"Nah, girl. I was just saying." They both laughed.

"Let me finish. I've been chattin' wit' this nigga on MySpace and now we're supposed to meet up. But, I don't wanna meet him by myself."

"Have you lost your fucking mind? What the hell are you doing wasting time on MySpace? Your ass is supposed to be working, not playing around on those people's computer." She knew that Cindy was on MySpace all the time because sometimes she checked MySpace from her laptop and Cindy's light would always be lit up.

"The state can kiss my ass. They don't pay me enough to entice me to become an exemplary employee. I stay on the computer: MySpace, BlackPlanet, Facebook, Match.com and Black Singles. I'm tryin' to find another damn husband. Anyways, like I was sayin'. I wanna meet this nigga, but I don't wanna go alone. You down or what? Oh, and the club is in Tampa, not slow, tired ass St. Pete."

"What club?" Tampa had some raunchy clubs too.

"It's the Blue Martini in International Plaza."

"Oh, I like that club. It's upscale and elite."

"I knew yo' bourgeois, snobbish ass would. So, you goin' or what?" she asked again.

"Yeah, I guess I'll go. I'm just not going to hang out all night. You know I have to be refreshed to teach a class full of kids."

"Hell, dealin' wit' them crumb snatchers ought to drive you to drinkin'."

"I know that's right. So, what time you coming or should I drive?" She knew how Cindy got. The woman could drink any man she knew under the table. And talk about getting buck wild and turning a club out. Lord have mercy.

"I'm drivin'. I promise to stick to two drinks. I don't wanna get too vulnerable. The guy might turn out to be an ax murder or somethin' and I might have to drop kick that nigga in the throat."

"Damn, sis. You can take the bitch out the hood, but you can't take the hood out the bitch."

"And you know that shit," she said matter-of-factly. "I'm Jordan Park projects in and out, all up and through." They had both grown up in the projects known as Jordan Park and had been friends since attending Jordan Park Elementary.

"Should I bring my pepper spray, just in case?"

"That watered down shit. You might as well just poke a bitch in the eye with two fingers." Greta heard a male's voice in the background. She assumed Cindy's husband had arrived home. "I'll be there between 9:30 and 10:00," Cindy said.

"Make it ten. That'll give me time to do something with my hair."

"You betta throw on a wig or slap on a drawstring ponytail like I do."

"I don't do the ponytails and wigs look too fake."

"Not the one I'm gonna wear."

"Which one is that? You got so many," she said sarcastically.

"Girl, I'm gonna pimp my Beverly Johnson, color #4, style Oprah," she stated matter-of-factly.

She had Greta rolling. "You are a trip. Girl, I will see you when you get here. Let me get off this phone and finish up these papers so I can get ready."

"Okay. And don't call my ass in thirty minutes sayin' you ain't goin'," she warned.

"I won't. I promise."

"Alright then. Bye."

"Bye."

***

"This club had better be jumping. You made me miss the last half hour of *Criminal Minds*," Greta told Cindy. They were just getting off the exit that would take them directly into International Plaza.

"You don't care nothin' 'bout that show. You just watch it to see Shemar Moore. He be wearin' the hell outta that FBI shirt and vest. That nigga is fione."

"Mouth-watering."

"Tasty."

"Scrumptious."

"Damn, you makin' me want some dick," Cindy exclaimed.

"You got Greg at home. You shouldn't ever be in need of dick."

"Ple-ease," she drugged the word out. "Why the hell you think I'm out here on the prowl? Greg has been havin' a little malfunction problem as of late."

"What? You mean his dick can't get hard? Don't lie."

"I'm dead ass serious. And the muthafucka won't go get a checkup. Talkin' 'bout his male pride."

"Well, what about you? Doesn't he care that he's not able to satisfy you?"

Cindy shrugged her narrow shoulders. "Apparently not enough to get a checkup."

"I know you want me to say that I understand. But, I don't. Cheating is never an option when you're married," Greta said seriously.

"Bitch, what the hell do you know?" She swung into a vacant parking space. "Your dried up ass need to get some damn dick. That shit is going to turn into the motherfucking Sahara Desert."

"How you know I didn't get some?" Greta replied hotly, gathering her purse and checking her hair in the mirror. Her heartbeat increased just from remembering her heated night of passion with the principal. She wasn't going to tell Cindy though.

"From who? You don't even date. You stay locked in the house. You rarely go anywhere. When did you find time to meet anybody? At church?" She whirled around to stare into her face. "Don't tell me you done fucked that fine ass pastor at that church you go to from time to time?"

"Girl, no. Don't I wish," she answered truthfully.

"Hell, I'd do him in a heartbeat. I bet he have all the women creamin' in their panties every Sunday."

"Now, you are going to hell for that one." Greta shook her head, chuckling. "He is devoted to God and by the look of things he's going to stay that way."

"Maybe he's gay and is just hiding behind the church."

"I don't know. He was married before and has children. Maybe he had a bad experience and that's what made him turn to God."

"A bitch can do that to a brother. We have some seriously deranged bitches in Da Burg, you hear me?" Cindy switched the car off and removed the keys from the ignition. "Well, this nigga better be here. Look for someone Hispanic, wearin' a black shirt and beige slacks. He says he'll have on a black Onyx ring."

"That could be any damn body."

"He's about five eight, with a nice body. He claims to be a body builder."

"Okay. Lead the way and I'll follow. Didn't he send you a picture?"

"Yeah, but that bitch was blurry. I couldn't really make out his features."

Greta just shook her head and followed Cindy into the club. They both wore form-fitting dresses that were sexy, but conservative. Neither of them wanted to advertise like they were gold-diggers or hookers.

When they entered, Greta looked around. The club's environment was more than satisfactory. On one side of the club they played hip-hop and they played Reggaeton on the other side. Cindy got into it right away after ordering a drink. She found her way to the center of the dance floor and started dancing like Halle Berry in the movie *BAPS*.

Greta was content to stand off to the side and watch. She sipped on some Seagram's and sprite. She saw a group of women crowded around a fine brother. From the way the women carried on, she figured he played for the Tampa Bay Buccaneers. Members of the team frequented The Blue Martini.

Whoever the player was, he appeared to be bewildered and uncomfortable. It wasn't long before he got up and left. The crowd of gold-diggers stood with their mouths wide open in shock.

"No he didn't," one of them said.

"He ain't all that."

"He must think his shit doesn't stink."

Greta found it all amusing. They needed to stop fronting. They were just mad because he wasn't interested in any of them.

"Hey, sexy," someone breathed against her earlobe. "Can I refresh that drink?" She turned to see Larry Newsome standing there.

"Hey, Larry." She smiled and gave him a quick hug. "I would let you buy me another one, but I think this is going to be it for tonight."

"Are you sure?"

Greta gazed out toward the dance floor and saw Cindy doing some stripper type dance. Where the hell had she learned that?

"I'm sure," she said. "I may have to drive home."

"Well, how about a dance later on?" Larry asked.

"I'll think about it, Lar," she said politely. She didn't want to turn him down flat. Larry was a nice guy. He was handsome, witty, and smart. She just didn't want to get involved with him and she could tell that he was more than a little interested in her. Why lead him on?

"I hope your answer will be yes," he said smoothly then walked off.

Greta put her empty glass onto the counter. A song by Akon and Snoop Dog blasted out the speakers and everybody in the club seemed to come alive. The dance floor went from semi-empty to overly-crowded in mere seconds.

I see you windin' and grindin' up on that pole. And I see you lookin' at me and you already know. I wanna fuck you.

"What?" Greta couldn't believe the lyrics blasting from the loud speakers. It seemed that the more vulgar the lyrics got, the more hype the crowd became. She knew there was a reason why she didn't frequent nightclubs anymore.

People were gyrating, bumping, grinding and pulling it down. They were popping, twirking and shaking everything God and their mamas gave them. It was just too much for her system to handle.

"Hey. Greta, I found him," Cindy said breathlessly, pulling on the arm of a very attractive Hispanic guy. "This is my best friend, Greta," she introduced. "Greta, this is Diego."

"Hello, Diego."

"Hello." They nodded at each other politely.

"Diego, I'll be right back." Cindy said, and pulled Greta in the direction of the bathroom because they couldn't carry on a conversation over the loud music.

"Girl, I gotta get wit' this fine ass man," she said. "He's gonna follow us home."

"What? You can't take him to your place. Isn't Greg home?"

"Yes Greg's flat foot ass is home. I know I can't take him there. I'm going to take you home and leave my car at your place. Then, me and Diego are leaving in his car and we gonna get a room."

"Cindy. Why don't you at least wait until you two go out a few times?" She hadn't waited to let Austin Johnson hit it. Who was she to try to tell her friend how long to wait to give her stuff up?

"Fuck that. I'm horny. Shit, do you realize that I haven't had any dick in damn near three months?"

"Shit. That's a long time. But-"

"I'm fuckin' him," Cindy cut in. "Period."

"Okay," Greta said lowly.

"So, are you ready to leave?" She checked her hair in the mirror and reapplied her lipstick.

"Sure. I might as well be."

"Don't have an attitude. You knew why I wanted to come here tonight," she reminded.

Greta gave a reluctant nod. "Okay. It's your business. Just be careful," she finally said.

"I will. I got the Trojans and the Magnums- just in case." She winked suggestively and Greta shook her head. "Now, let me get back to that fine motherfucker before some skank snatches him up." They headed out of the ladies' room. "Hey, isn't that Larry?" Greta turned to look where Cindy pointed.

"Yeah, I spoke to him earlier. He wanted to get a dance before I left. I guess he'll have to wait on that another time."

"I don't know why you don't get wit' him. He'd probably be good for you. Y'all have similar interests," Cindy said.

"I don't know. There's just something about him that I can't quite put my finger on."

They rejoined Diego at the bar. Cindy slipped her arms around the lucky man. Greta could admit that Diego was quite handsome and even though small in stature, his body was chiseled. When he finished his drink, the three of them headed for the exit.

As Greta, Cindy and her newfound friend left the club, Larry stared behind them. His face tightened and he got a strange look in his eye. Suddenly, he slammed the glass he'd been drinking from onto the counter top.

Trifling bitches. They are all alike.

"Sir, would you like another drink?" The bartender asked nervously.

"No. I'm good." He gave her a cold look. "What you doing after you get off?"

"I'm engaged," she said, wiggling her left hand and the ring in the air. She quickly turned her attention to another customer.

"As if that matters," Larry muttered. "Married, engaged, in a relationship—that shit don't matter. If a bitch wants to fuck, a bitch is gonna get some outside dick."

www.ingramcontent.com/pod-product-compliance
Lightning Source LLC
Chambersburg PA
CBHW011520240626

47154CB00009B/2906